PnPAuthors and Poets: Peter & Pattimari Cacciolfi, Deepak Menon, Kathryn Treat, Christopher Meade, Sayed Rohani, Marie Lavender, Alfancena, Phibby Venable, Dawn Huffaker, Charles Ray, James Horn, Marlowe Sr., Eve Gaal

Short Stories & Poems

By

PnPAuthors

Authors will have their names under
the short story and poem they wrote.

ISBN:

978-1-312-38221-3

A LINGERING FRAGRANCE –winner of the contest

By *Deepak Menon*

The dog's erratic course found him standing once again outside her house. His drooping and soft brown eyes gazed longingly at the verandah, seeming to will the forbiddingly large opaque door of the house to open.

Within, the lady of the house busied herself with those seemingly endless household chores, which constituted the basic aim of her existence. She had been working tirelessly with a blank, automated, compulsive mind for some time now.

The dog continued in fits and starts, to sniff around in circles, always returning to his station just inside the compound where, after a pause to gaze at the door of the house, he would resume his aimless wandering.

Though it is difficult to say why, the lady of the house, whom we shall call 'Faith', for want of a better name, started abruptly, just as she was about to begin ironing the umpteenth garment for the day. Her eyes flickered to the clock. It was 9 A.M. hurriedly switching off the Iron, she made her way to the door, and opening it, stepped out into the verandah. Her anxious eyes searched wildly around for an instant, before coming to rest on the forlorn figure of the dog, waiting patiently at his self-appointed station.

She stepped out into the compound, and the dog, with a whimper of pure joy, raced towards her coming to a skidding stop at her feet. A smile suddenly illuminated her face. The wrinkles of care and worry vanished as if they had never been. The dog too, had changed. The perceptible droop in his bearing had been replaced with a marked hauteur. Her hand dropped down to his downy head and her fingers caressed his soft ears. The dog, (who had no name) wagged his tail furiously, and rubbed his flanks against her legs. She knelt down and placing both arms around his neck, hugged him close to her breast. And there they remained for some immeasurable time that may have been a moment or an hour - no one can tell. It was the perfect communion of contented, selfless, devotion between the two, incredibly beautiful to behold for one who KNOWS.

By and by, she loosened her embrace, for the dog, though quite breathless with her frenetically tight grasp, was yet loath to let it end. It would have been very clear to any person who knows about these things, that the dog would have willingly died in her arms, with no other regret than the regret that he could not suffer a thousand more such deaths. However, such people, as we all know, are few and far between.

The only person, who observed the meeting between the two, was the sharp-tongued housewife in the house across the street, who wrinkled her nose in disgust. She did so, not because she was motivated by any hatred of dogs or harboured any ill will against her neighbour. She wrinkled her nose in disgust simply because she was not one of those, who KNOWS.

She saw not the unutterable beauty of the emotions behind the embrace. She saw only that the woman was dressed in a nightdress quite unsuitable for stepping outdoors in, and that the dog was a Mongrel with a half-starved look and a ragged muddy and mangy coat, probably suffering from a large percentage of known dog diseases, and probably many as yet unknown to man.

However, her opinion hardly mattered to either the woman or the dog (at least at that moment), for both were oblivious to the world, and probably would not have noticed the wrinkled nose even if it had been hovering an inch from their faces. The piercing whistle of the pressure cooker sliced down like a guillotine, in a fraction of an instant severing into two, their molded bodies. Hastily slipping a biscuit into the dog's mouth, the lady hurried into the house, never looking back. The dog stood there a moment, during which time he allowed the magic that had transformed him into a majestic creature, to evaporate. Slowly turning, he dragged his once again drooping tail away.

One may have been mistaken, but hardly had he taken a few steps, it appeared as if some thought, (possibly of tomorrows tryst) entered his mind, and once again his bearing became erect and his tail straightened as he vanished into the distance. Of course, it must have been the imagination of the observer.

For, *who ever heard of a thinking dog?* The dog had entered the woman's life quite imperceptibly. She never knew quite since when, but had a dim recollection of seeing the dog often standing at his self-appointed station, but could not exactly say when she actually noticed him. As for the dog, it is quite obviously pointless to speculate as to why or how he came to get into the habit of standing outside the woman's house, despite the fact that there was no earthly reason for him to do so.

One may possibly presume, that there was an unearthly or supernatural reason, but that is quite ridiculous, for he was only a stray dog, such as are found in the droves and dozens all around the world; and it would be equally impossible for us to imagine that the dog had planned the entire thing to gain the woman's confidence, for dogs, as we all know, live for the moment and are incapable of preparing for the future, being of simple trusting minds. Let us therefore leave the motives or reasons to the 'Seers' to determine. Suffice it then to say, he had simply started coming there.

The days passed. The daily ritual continued. The woman became the subject of talk as often happens when people are not able to comprehend actions they themselves cannot associate with.

The woman's family found her actions impossible to understand, especially when the daily ritual with the dog interfered with their lives. The entire family planned a holiday. The woman, however, delayed their departure on the appointed day on some pretext or the other till the dog appeared. Despite the panic of departure, she took a moment off to hug the dog and pass on a handful of biscuits. Then she was off in the car with never a backward glance, listening to the reproduction of her family, leaving the dog staring forlornly after her. The train was boarded only in the nick of time.

We can only presume why she did this. Maybe because she had no way to tell the dog that she was going out of town, and she felt that he would understand only if she went in his presence. It would be quite silly to think that she whispered her itinerary to the dog while she hugged him. But, strange as it may seem, it was observed (and sworn before several of the communities honored and honest gossips, to be the truth) by the woman with the perpetually wrinkled nose across the street, that the dog only put in his next appearance the morning after Faith returned.

And then, one day, when the dog arrived for his "daily dose of life", the manner of the woman had changed. She threw him a biscuit, and without even kneeling to hug him, she hurried back into the house. Who knows what the dog must have felt, but later, when she came out into the verandah, she noticed the biscuit laying untouched where the dog had stood. A flicker of a teardrop glistened momentarily in her eyes, but then resolutely she tore her gaze away from the biscuit, and went back into the house. Her shoulders, however, were slightly hunched.

The next morning Faith did not open the door. The dog took his appointed place, and stood for a long time, all the while appearing to shrink into himself, before slowly (very slowly) crawling away like a beaten cur. Here it may be said; a smile crossed the usually straight and tight lips of the woman in the window across the street, though we have no way of really telling why. And through a narrow split in the curtains, Faith watched him go, through swollen eyelids.

The very next morning, when the dog arrived, Faith was already at the gate. She ran to him and hugged him so hard that his bones creaked. She wept tears (of happiness or repentance one cannot say). And finally, when she returned to the house, one could have observed, if one had been there, the sudden radiance in the woman and the sudden royal bearing of the dog as he stalked away. For some time everything continued as always. And then the break in the ritual occurred again. The whole charade was enacted again, with all the immense sadness of separation and the incredible joy of union. But it could have been observed that, while the woman was strong enough to not only initiate the break, but continue it till the final bell, the dog was not. Back he came again and again and again.

If only one could see into the dog's mind, one would be able to fathom the way he thought. One who has had experience with dogs, may be quite sure that the dog could not understand what was happening. For dogs have simple minds, and their devotion never varies.

As to whether the dog felt hurt, and then too, how badly, is again a matter for conjecture. It can be thought that the dog did not feel very badly hurt because he always came back to the woman, possibly for the biscuit. But if one considers the gradual general decline of the dog, and the fact, that whenever he sensed indifference in the woman, he left the biscuit untouched, one may construe the earlier explanation to be incorrect.

Whatever the truth may be, the dog's devotion was total and complete despite his puzzlement, hurt, or sadness. With time, the behavior of Faith became even more erratic, alternating between fits of delirious joy at meeting the dog, to tearful fits of cruelty aimed at driving the dog away. Her reasons for doing this, she kept to herself. If one could have peered into her heart, one may have seen the excruciating pain arising from the fear of some impending disaster such as separation. It may be that paradoxically, instead of grappling the dog (who had come to symbolize all sorts of noble things to her) to her heart, she strove to lessen the shock of the actual event by driving him away before. But this is in many ways, a Love Story. And Dogs devotions never vary. Even unto death. So it cannot be expected that the dog would ever default in his sole aim of existence. But that is what he did one day, many months after the housewife had completely stopped coming to the door when he came. He did not appear at his station that day. Nor the next. Or the next...

Epilogue:-

I was the woman. And I loved the dog with a passion that was spiritual in its intensity.

I could not adopt the dog because my family would have none of it. And I, valuing my family, yet torn apart by my longing for the innocent devotion of those brown eyes, sacrificed him, and myself.

For weeks and then for months after he stopped coming, I found myself at the window every morning staring blankly at the spot where he used to sit. And then we moved away. But his memory never faded.

I would often think of what must have happened to him. Did he meet with an accident and die desolate and unattended? Or did he sense my sorrow and stop coming to spare me more pain? But either way, I was wrong. My pain did not lessen.

One day, grown strong with the passage of years, with the scoffs of my friends and family ringing in my ears, I traveled a thousand miles back to the lingering fragrance of his Love. *And planted a rose in his memory at the sacred spot!*

A Holiday Romance with a Difference
by Christopher Antony Meade

The highlight of my visit to Transylvania last year was my meeting with the very handsome young Ferdinand and the visit to his castle, situated on a rocky promontory, in the foothills of the Carpathian Mountains. I can still recall the graceful way he almost floated up the steps that led to the dark heavy door of his fortress home. The gleaming whiteness of his, oh so sharp, teeth when he smiled is still a happy recollection. I really did feel like I was a great lady coming home when he gave a sweeping bow as he welcomed me across his ancient threshold.

I had been staying in a rather boring concrete box like hotel, which dated from the Communist era and was considered the best accommodation for tourists in that out of the way district. The comrades might have considered it to be the height of luxury, but I had a longing to experience the more authentic side of Transylvania, so when the gorgeous young man, sitting next to me in the restaurant, told me that the castle, sitting glowering down on the village from its limestone crag, was his home, I eagerly accepted his invitation to stay overnight.

So there I was two hours later sipping a glass of the deepest red wine as we sat opposite each other by the blazing fire in the Great Hall. Portraits of ancestors, in costumes going back to the 14th century, gazed down on us as my host chatted animatedly about the attractions he was determined to show me, in the local area. Even though I was getting slightly tipsy, I did notice that the dust seemed to sit a bit too much on most surfaces within the room. There seemed to be an absence of servants and I noticed that he brought the wine and glasses into the room himself, rather than ring for somebody to serve it. I was too politely brought up to make comment, however, besides what's a little dust between friends?

After we chatted amiably, for what must have been two or three hours, my growing more handsome by the minute companion, asked me if I would like to be shown to my bedroom. I had been anticipating an invitation to his chamber, but I comforted myself with the notion that he might come to my room after I had retired, so I readily agreed to his suggestion. I noticed again the cobwebs and the dust that bestrewed the wide staircase leading to the upper floors. The servants were either very lazy or they didn't exist. I was informed that as I was a special guest, I would be staying in the Count's room. The Count apparently was a 19th century ancestor and his portrait adorned the very special quilt on the big four-poster bed. A tremor of excitement agitated my being, when I considered that I would be spending the night in such august splendour.

My, oh so HOT, companion bowed again as he left me outside the bedroom door. I was eagerly anticipating his return as I switched on the lights to survey the room. For a change, there was no dust. Indeed the welcoming smell of furniture polish wafted to my surprised nostrils. Against the wall opposite the door was an immense four-poster bed, the perfect place I thought for investigating whether ancient lineage came with great potency. When I looked at the portrait that was embroidered on the quilt, all notions of fun and games evaporated right away.

Staring up at me was the figure of a man lying in a coffin. The embroiderer's skill must have been great indeed. Scarlet thread had been skillfully used to show the trickle of blood coming from the snarling mouth and the hands seemed to almost reach out to grasp me, as I stared in transfixed horror at the monstrosity I was expected to have as my bedfellow. What really scared me was the realisation that, although the face before me was distorted by savage rage, there was still a very strong resemblance to the young man who had charmed me by the fireside earlier that evening. My feelings of lustful anticipation rapidly dissolved, to be replaced by dreadful forebodings, when I remembered hearing a key being turned in the lock just after

I'd entered the room. As I said at the beginning, the high point of my holiday in Transylvania was meeting the very handsome Count Ferdinand. The low point was discovering that his surname was Dracula.

Our Forest of Dreams - SONNET NO 1 by Deepak Menon

SONNET NO 1 by Deepak Menon

A cry of yearning when escapes my anguished lips

To break the stillness of the velvet night of the past

And pain from my wounded heart into mine conscious rips

To awaken those moments of an eternity that did not last

Then dost thou come alive within me in that timeless form

That I have forgotten existed like an ephemeral spark

Then dost lightning flash illumining the nameless swarm

Of deep buried memories like wisps out of the dark

To smooth my furrowed brow some blissful while

To salve that open wound with the herb that heals

To bring back the flicker of that enchanted smile

Turning back to the beginning of time, Fortune's wheels

And the golden glory of creation surrounds me once more

As we fade away into the Forest of Dreams - evermore.

Tales of Love, written by Sayed H. Rohani

Have you seen the two birds' beaks touching each other?

Have you seen the two swans hugging each other?

Have you seen the moths roasting on the glittering flames?

Have you seen the plants putting forth young shoots?

They are all telling of love.

Have you seen the charm of the gazing eyes?

Have you seen the tearful desirous eyes?

Have you seen the two lips touching each other?

Have you seen the two faces pressed together?

They are all telling of love.

Have you seen the swan dancing lithely to give vent to his

emotions?

Have you seen the nightingale singing of loneliness?

Have you seen the dove cooing on his love?

Have you seen the crickets singing in the dark?

They are all telling of love.

Have you seen the penguins suffering intense pain to meet their

fledglings?

Have you seen the turtles making a long journey to safeguard

their hatchlings?

Have you seen does sacrificing themselves to protect their fawns?

Have you seen mammals licking their newborns?

They are all telling of love.

Have you seen those heroes risking their lives to rescue lives?

Have you seen those heroes cheering up the melancholy orphans?

Have you seen those heroes battling fires to help the sufferers?

Have you seen those heroes using their lives as bulwarks to save

the liberties?

They are all telling of love.

Have you seen the clouds thundering?

Have you seen the lightening dazzling?

Have you seen the wind blowing?

Have you seen the mountains echoing?

They are all telling of love.

Have you seen those feeding the hungry?

Have you seen those uplifting the desperate?

Have you seen those sheltering the homeless?

Have you seen those sharing others' sorrows?

They are all telling of love.

 Have you seen the oceans rising?

Have you seen the rivers roaring?

Have you seen the springs whispering?

Have you seen the lakes rippling and sparkling?

They are all telling of love.

Have you seen hearts filled with compassion?

Have you seen souls gifted with humanity?

Have you seen deeds given to magnanimity?

Have you seen habits disposed to civility?

They are all telling of love.

Have you seen the electrons moving around their nucleus?

Have you seen the planets orbiting around the sun?

Have you seen the galaxies rotating around their centers?

Have you seen the universe singing the praise of its Creator?

They are telling of love.

The Life and Death of a Lady. A Picture of an Aristocratic Life

By Christopher Antony Mease

The Elderly Aristocrat

The old woman felt that the stairs were getting increasingly difficult to negotiate in recent years. Perhaps it might make more sense to sleep downstairs now that rheumatism was attacking her knees, as well as the arthritis that was starting to twist her once beautiful fingers into claws that would have looked better on an eagle than on a human being. Still, she would continue to make the effort. If she could sleep in her own room, rather than bedding down on a camp bed in front of the fire in the old servants' hall, she could feel that the old days were not entirely gone, and she was still Lady Margaret Davenshaw, rather than just the just creaking old "bag of bones", who would certainly not see ninety again.

An Aristocratic Life

Lady Margaret was no snob, and she had always been kind to the servants in the days when she had them. She was not like her parents. They had been so grand that they would not even notice if a maid or a footman was in the room. They had carried on private conversations, and sometimes arguments, at dinner while taking no regard to whether the person pouring the soup could hear every word. To her parents, an on duty servant was just a utensil, not much different really than a tray with legs. That had been the time when Edward VII had been on the throne. In the years before World War One everyone knew their place, and they were content with it.

In the years following that great conflict there had been some changes. So many of the footmen that had stood to attention in their knee breeches, and made sure no member of the family ever needed to pull in their own chair, had fallen foul of German machine gunners, that some changes had to be made. So many maids had also found that there was more money and freedom to be got from working in factories than from combing a lady's hair, or dusting the Louis Quinze furniture, that female servants were increasingly difficult to retain. Lady Margaret's mother actually met her end when she forgot that the conveniences of a lifetime were no longer there. She fell and broke her hip when she attempted to sit down for dinner, while forgetting that there no longer was a survivor to push in her chair. Old Lord Davenshaw only survived the death of his wife by around nine months. Since there was no male heir, Davenshaw Manor became the property of Lady Margaret. The staff, that had numbered over sixty indoor and outdoor servants, was reduced to around fifteen to look after all departments of the estate.

That was one of the reasons why the new chatelaine had a more informal relationship with her household staff. She was still the mistress, and the time honoured conventions were still largely observed. Everybody called her "Madame" or "Ma'am". Maids would curtsy to her, and the male servants would always give a little bow.

They would continue to stand up when she entered a room where they were. Unlike her parents, she would ask them to sit down again straight away. In the years before the war, no servant would ever be addressed by their first name. They were always Jones or Grimshaw or whatever the surname might be. One footman, who was blessed with the name Davenshaw, was required to change his name to Reynolds, as it was considered unsuitable for a "livery" to have the same nomenclature as the family.

This name nonsense was swept away by the time the nineteen twenties dawned. Lady Margaret knew everybody's first name, and she always used it. Except for the butler, who remained Mr. Sharpington, the cook who was Mrs. Greaves, and the housekeeper Mrs. Roscoe. The old snobberies lingered longer "downstairs", than they were allowed to in the salons of the house above. Sometimes there would be parties like in the old days. But extra agency servants would have to be brought in specially, as the smaller permanent staff could not be expected to cope with the additional workload.

Lady Margaret never married. The guns of The Kaiser had taken as much toll on the upper classes as they had on the footmen and gardeners. So there were just not enough suitable gentlemen around to wed all the aristocratic young "hopefuls". A son of a newspaper magnate did express an interest, but his suit did not prosper. He was just not of the right class to be marrying a lady who could trace her ancestors back to the twelfth century. He later allied his millions with an American from New Hampshire, (a much more suitable match for him really).

When the Second World War broke out in 1939 Davenshaw Manor was converted into a convalescent home for soldiers that had been wounded in the service of King and Country. The Louis Quinze furniture was stored in the stable wing, and iron framed beds and comfortable sofas took its place in all the grand rooms. Lady Margaret, who was now in her early forties, used to come round and sit by the soldiers' beds to listen to their stories of battles fought and sweethearts left behind. She sometimes had to speak comforting words to them when the same sweethearts wrote to break off relations because they could not face the prospect of being tied to crippled life partners. Talking to the soldiers, and mixing with the nurses and the doctors who staffed the home, gave the lady of the manor a greater insight into the lives led by the legions of ordinary people that she would have only encountered before when they were serving at her table or laying out her clothes for some grand ball or other. Her attitude towards those, she once thought as her inferiors, moved even further from the lofty disdain felt by her parents. She never ceased to be "the Lady" though. The consciousness of rank was just too embedded in her being in that. Those around her still felt it about her and, even though the world was being turned upside down by war, most of the old courtesies of position were still observed. She might call a nurse or a housemaid Mabel or Kate, but they still all addressed her as "Your Lady-ship", or Lady Margaret. It was just that a new kindness started to underline all the old practices.

Time and Tide Wait for no Man, or Aristocratic Lady

After the war in the nineteen fifties, the staffing levels in the great house were reduced even more than they had been in the twenties and thirties. Work that had once been done by seven housemaids was now done by a "daily" with a vacuum cleaner. Electric heaters replaced the coal fires, thus reducing the need for staff even more. Mr. Sharpington died and the position of butler died with him. When Mrs. Greaves and Mrs. Roscoe retired to live out their lives at the seaside, there were no more resident servants left to call Lady Margaret "Madame", or even "Ma'am".

Age came upon Lady Margaret Davenshaw, even as the dust accumulated on the Louis Quinze furniture and the weeds started to choke out the flowers in the overgrown gardens of Davenshaw Manor. Some investments that she had made in Argentinian lead mine shares had failed very badly and a large portion of the family estate had been sold to pay off the banks. By the nineteen eighties, even the "daily" with the vacuum was a thing of the past. The lady of the manor lived entirely on her own. One concession had been made to the modern age. There was a telephone system with extensions on every floor, and on the landings. These had been installed on the urgings of Mrs. Roscoe, who had visited her old mistress and been appalled by the conditions that she found her living in. "At least this way you can call for help, your Lady-ship, if you have an emergency" the concerned old servitor had said.

This brings us back to the start of our story. The very old Lady Margaret was making her way slowly from the servants 'hall, which was the sole room she occupied during the day to her old bedroom on the second floor. But the stairs, which were not very well maintained these days, had a loose board. This night the old lady stepped on the neglected timber, which shot up and propelled her back down a flight of stairs. Her ninety three year old left leg made a cracking sound as it fractured. The pain was agonising. She did just manage to drag herself over to the landing telephone and call an ambulance. When the paramedics arrived, they had to break down the big front door to gain access. When they asked her name she faintly said "Lady Margaret Davenshaw". They called her "Margaret".

At the hospital, after her leg had been plastered, she was put into an iron framed bed in a ward that included male and female patients. Lady Margaret had never shared a sleeping room with a man in

Her entire life. Now she had old men with open backed hospital gowns coming over to her bed to stare at her. The nurses were kind, and they did their best to see that all their patients were comfortable. But they did not know anything of the old courtesies. They called her "Margaret". One of them even addressed her as "Marge".

The elderly deserve their dignity. They have earned it

It is a problem often found in the modern world, that people are too much addicted to addressing each other by their first name. When I was growing up the rule was that a married woman was always referred to as Mrs., unless you had gone to school with her, or she was a relative. Then you could call her "Margaret" or "Kate", or whatever. It was an accepted convention, and as such everyone was comfortable with its use. Now, in our over democratic age, everybody tries to be friendly first, and fewer people get addressed with the old formality.
This often causes problems for the elderly, and is especially irksome to them when they are ill or in hospital. A lady or a gentleman, who have all their lives been used to being called Mrs. or Mr. Jones, can feel profoundly uncomfortable and stripped of dignity, when they find themselves called "Gertie" or "Stan" by some over familiar stranger who is giving them a bed bath.

This is the situation that Lady Margaret found herself in. As I said previously, she had never been a snob. Indeed kindness and the consideration of the feelings and welfare of others had always been a feature of her character. The house by the sea that Mrs. Roscoe and Mrs. Greaves had retired to had been a gift from her. But she had been brought up, and lived all her life, as a lady. The shock of being routinely addressed in a manner that she felt stripped her of dignity, brought on feelings of depression that left her unable to fight when a hospital borne infection assailed her frail body within a week of admission. The last words she heard before slipping into the final coma were "poor old Maggie can't have long to go now". It was the ward sister who was talking to a staff nurse.

Afternoon in the Garden

By Christopher

Behind him the noise escalated as the deadly predator came rapidly nearer. He froze in terror as there seemed little point in trying to get away. The underfoot vegetation provided too slippery a surface for his trembling feet to get a grip. Besides his fat body could only trundle along. He was starting to bitterly regret the urge to eat and eat, that had got him into his present terrifying predicament. It had started out as a normal day in the garden. The sun was shining and all the family cheerfully set about their daily routine of stripping the leaves from the blooming cabbage plants. All his ancestors, for countless generations, had worked at the same business. They had prospered at it and would continue to do so while nature provided its bounty for their sustenance. There were enemies in the garden, however. Nobody could guarantee that the working day might not be cut fatally short. There was always that dreadful risk. The safest thing really was to congregate together. A large contingent might confuse a predator or, if the worst came to the worst and there was an attack, at least the chance of an individual to survive was increased. To get separated from your family, in such a dangerous environment, could be like signing your own death warrant. Just like lions will single out the lone antelope for the evening dinner, the hunters that patrolled this workplace were always on the lookout for stragglers. It was a deadly lack of judgment on his part, to linger over some extra scrumptious leaf remnants, when the rest of the industrious family had moved off. It was only when he heard the distant flapping that he became conscious of his deadly peril. Looking up, he realized, with a feeling of dread, that he was alone and probably facing his last moments alive. The noise continued to escalate until his terrified consciousness registered nothing except its terrifying cacophony.

The bird swooped down and one peck replaced his absolute terror with total oblivion. The caterpillar would never become a butterfly now.

The Missing Piece

By Marie Lavender

Angelica Masters woke up slowly. The sun was directly overhead, spilling its yellow glow over her face and arms. She stretched, feeling the soreness envelop every part of her body. She sat up and propped her elbows on her knees. She blinked quickly, trying to remember why she was lying in the grass. From the edges of her memory came a hazy picture of a party scene.

It was a large, but crowded room. The smell of alcohol permeated the air and several people were milling about, talking or dancing together. A guy with dark blonde hair and a lanky build brushed past her and toppled over a nearby coffee table while gales of laughter erupted nearby. The picture faded and she tried to find a reason why she might attend such an event. It wasn't her kind of scene.

Angelica was a recluse. She had been accused of it many times and she wouldn't deny it. The things her roommates did had never held any appeal for her. She was perfectly happy if she sat at home, reading a great novel rather than attend the weekend parties Kylie and Karen, the two girls who lived with her, were known for visiting. She didn't want to make waves like them. She wasn't prepared to venture into the dating scene like everyone else. She actually preferred her own company to that of the male persuasion. They all seemed so caught up in the weekend scene and were so full of themselves that it was probably better if she avoided them altogether. She remembered how her roommates had begged her to go to the party the night before. No matter what ploy they used, no matter what they did to try to persuade her that it might be worth going to, she had refused. She had also advised them that if they had any common sense, they wouldn't go on such a suicide mission. There was too much to risk.

"You must be jealous," Kylie retorted. "You think we might get lucky and you won't."

Measuring up to her roommates' experience was the last thing Angelica wanted. They constantly teased her about her virginity. To her, keeping it was more sacred than trying to give it away to a complete stranger. Last night, she had let Karen and Kylie leave without giving them a reply. And yet it made no sense that she had memories, although vague, of a party she had attended. It was also worth questioning why she happened to be lying on the lawn of the nearest fraternity house. It was morning, nine o'clock by her watch Sunday. Thank God it was a weekend or she would have missed a class.

"Hello?"

She jerked her head up to see a tall boy in black jeans and a blue shirt. Narrowing her eyes, she asked, "What do you want?"

He frowned as if surprised by her stinging reply. "I just wondered if you were all right. That was some party last night."

"I suppose so."

He kneeled to her level. "You don't remember?" She looked down to see that she was wearing a bright pink shirt and white capris with brown sandals. The outfit was certainly not from her wardrobe, which usually consisted of jeans and plain t-shirts. She looked up at him again. She could tell him about the memory, but she preferred to find out the truth first. "I don't. What was I doing there? Why did I go?" She became aware that she was speaking fast.

"Calm down. You're just confused. You drank a little last night. That's all."

"I never drink. Alcohol, that is."

"I see." He suddenly looked uncertain and she wondered what he was thinking.

"What happened to me?"

"I don't know. One of my friends, Brendan, talked to you a little. You hung out. I say you go upstairs with him. That's all. And now you're here."

He frowned again, rubbing his chin absently. She shuddered, her eyes wide on his face. "I went to a room alone with him?"

He sighed. "I don't know. You could assume that, but I guess you'd have to ask him. Are you all right?" he asked, touching her shoulder gently.

"No. I don't remember any of this. I might have-"she stopped, her hand raised to her mouth.

"Don't worry so much. Brendan's a good guy. He would never hurt anyone, especially a girl."

"How do you know?"

"I just know him."

It was enough for now, but that wasn't all she had to worry about. There were diseases and unwanted pregnancy. She clenched her fists. Certainly if she had gone that far with someone, she would have remembered. "I, I have to go home. I shouldn't be here." She sure felt as if she'd been mauled, but that could have been the effects of drinking as well.

"Okay. Can I walk you there?"

She studied his face. He seemed genuinely concerned about her. "If you like," she answered. He helped her to stand as she was a bit unsteady on her feet at first, and they walked away from the fraternity in silence for a while. She didn't know him and yet he had approached her to see if she was all right. Could he be trusted? "I never got your name…"

He glanced at her, grinning. "My name's Justin."

He has dimples, she mused. "I'm Angelica."

"That's a nice name."

"Thanks. I really go by Angie, at least to people I know pretty well." *Idiot.* She needed to hold onto her tongue more. She felt like she was babbling nervously when she would normally clam up with complete strangers. She cleared her throat. "Anyway, do you know how I could get hold of your friend Brendan? I really need to find out about last night."

He shrugged. "He sort of took off this morning; didn't say anything. He wasn't in his room and his car was missing. I assume he's running errands or something."

"You're not close?"

"We're good friends, but he's very independent. We all are. We pretty much live together only. We don't keep tabs on each other."

"Oh."

"If he was leaving town, he would have said it or left a note. That much we do."

"So I probably won't get any answers out of your buddies then."

"They all saw you last night, Angie. I just don't know how much they remember." He sighed. "Look, I'll do some checking around, see what I can find out about where Brendan went and also see if the guys remember what happened with you two."

"That would be helpful. Thanks."

"No problem. Hey, I'm just as worried as you about how you ended up outside when I saw you at the party last night. That's pretty strange."

"I know."

When he dropped her back at the dorms, she thanked him and went inside. As she trudged down the long hallway to the door at the end of the hall, she couldn't help thinking that her presence at a wild party would only affect her reputation; her actions there could even affect her college career. She didn't feel all that different, but a change could have certainly occurred while she was under the influence of alcohol. The uncertainty frightened her most of all.

****

All through her Biology class the next day, Angelica could not get her mind off of the party on Saturday night. What had actually happened? Who was the guy she'd been with? Had she made a terrible mistake by taking one risk in her life? She was not prone to taking such risks, at least not the kind with serious implications. Her most adventurous whims stemmed from a need to experience nature on a personal level. This usually included taking walks on campus at night. In her hometown, she often drove to the park to walk on the trails there. Her legs had grown accustomed to the rough, uneven paths through the forest and she often set large goals for herself, such as trekking for long distances through the foliage for most of the day. Her adventurous spirit as far as nature was concerned didn't cause her anxiety. The land was safe and she was confident in her own abilities to make the long treks. Even though she also knew the risks that her drive to see nature took her to, it worried her that the lengths her adventurous side had gone to were extreme, at least in terms of that party. That was the only conclusion she could come to about her reasons for being there. Surely she had to have gone to show Karen and Kylie that she was just as capable of having fun, but also to prove that parties were a lot more than the typical college experience. She had always tried to keep up with her studies and never take too many chances socially. She saw what bad choices did to people. They wound up confused about their actions and torn between right and wrong. She didn't want her one faulty decision to have needless repercussions. She would not tell her roommates. If they hadn't noticed her at the party, it was better that they didn't know about it. Angelica was certain they would either consider her an equally wild girl or laugh at her dilemma when they'd probably never worry about being with a complete stranger. That was a natural occurrence, but not for her.

"Okay, that's all for today. Read chapter six. Prepare for a quiz next time."

Dazed, Angelica picked up her books and stuffed them into her backpack. Slinging it over her shoulder, she left the room and headed for Granger Hall, the dorm complex in which she lived. She shook her head. It wasn't at all like her to miss a lecture. She needed to snap out of it and get her life back on track. When she reached the room, she opened the door, dropped her bag on the floor and slumped onto her bed. Why couldn't life hand you a pocket full of opportunity when you needed it? Why was it so complicated?

Disgusted, she grabbed a hair clip and pulled the pile of her tousled auburn locks into a bun and clipped it in place. She felt less of a bum. But, why was she trying? Had she done that much to improve her appearance the night of the party? She couldn't remember that either, but she must have tried to look different or she wouldn't have woken up in Kylie's outfit, which had been returned discreetly and unscathed. Why would she try so hard to be unlike herself?

An insistent knock on the door brought a sigh out of her. When she opened it, she saw Justin standing there in an awkward sort of way, both feet turned to the side in an anxious manner. "Oh, hi."

"Hi."

"Is there a problem?"

"No. Not at all. I was just around and I wondered if you might want to come and meet some of the guys, maybe ask them about the party. It might shed some light on the subject."

She shifted uncertainly. "Uh, I'll feel kind of strange. I thought you were going to ask."

"I was. But, I figured you needed answers right away. Besides, I think they'll give you more information. What happened with you and Brendan shouldn't really be any of my business although I do want to help."

He had a good point. Addressing the issue from his standpoint would be awkward indeed. He had nothing to do with it at all, but his willingness to help touched her. She released a pent-up breath. "All right, I'll go."

A half hour later, she found herself in a mad house. At the fraternity, dozens of guys walked back and forth, snacking on potato chips or they hung in groups, joking around with their buddies. A couple of them were throwing darts while another drank a beer wholly as if Saturday night's libations weren't enough. She looked over at Justin with a raised eyebrow.

"Don't worry. It won't be that bad."

She nodded. She had a hard time believing it when every guy in the house other than Justin seemed to ignore her presence. Before she was ready, he had led one over to them.

"Angelica, this is Barry. Angie was at the party on Saturday. She has a few questions for you."

"That's cool."

Grimacing, she began, "Uh, Barry, do you remember seeing anything on Saturday? With Brendan and me?"

He stroked his shadowed chin for a moment. "You guys went upstairs. I figured you were gonna get down. You know; the wild thing. It got pretty wild, didn't it?"

Angelica felt frozen to that spot in the carpet. It was as if all eyes were drawn to her, expecting some kind of response. It was like she was an abstract painting in a gallery which no one could tear their eyes from. They would just stand there, their heads tilted, content to spend a lifetime trying to figure out its meaning. She was sure she turned a shade of red, then, perhaps even scarlet. "Uh, I don't know." She looked to Justin for help.

He cleared his throat. "Come on, man. Leave her alone. Did Brendan say anything before he left Sunday?"

"No, man. He's so secretive, sometimes. It's been awhile for him, I'm sure. He wouldn't let a thing on to anyone. But, you saw them as clear as I did. They were all over each other. And she was dancing as sexy as hell."

What if she had slept with Brendan? She didn't even know the guy. Barry's description was not helping her. She felt as if she'd lose her breakfast at any minute. She didn't even dance. To think she had been all over some guy she didn't even know, it was so unreal. "I-I'm sorry. I can't-"

Then, she turned away and left the house. On the lawn, she tried to breathe slowly to prevent the knot from rising in her throat.

"Hey, are you all right?" Justin was at her side in what seemed like seconds.

She shook her head.

"Can you breathe okay?" At her response, he touched her shoulder. "Just focus on breathing. Don't think about anything else." After her breathing had slowed down, he sighed. "You panicked, that's all."

"Really? You're a genius."

He frowned.

She shrugged. "What if I did do that with him? Everything he said…none of that is like me. It doesn't make sense."

"Maybe you liked Brendan."

"I wouldn't act like that."

"How do you know how you would act in that situation?"

"I don't. But, I'm usually smarter than that. I wouldn't just do that with anyone, someone I don't know."

"That makes sense. But, maybe it wasn't as bad as you think."

"What are you saying?"

"I don't see the problem. Maybe it wasn't that bad at all."

"You wouldn't understand. You're used to that kind of life, sleeping with utter strangers and all; Taking risks."

He lifted a brow. "Angelica, I only mean that I don't understand why you're upset. Brendan can be trusted. And he's not the type you're talking about. He hasn't been with many women."

"How can you know that?"

"He's my friend."

"And you're ridiculously loyal!" As she turned away, he grabbed her arm so that she faced him. He was very close now, too close for comfort. She shivered in an odd response.

"I'm not taking sides," he said softly. "I just know him. That's the only reason I can give you to keep you from freaking out. I can assure you he's a good guy. That's all. I can't prove it. I just know."

"It's hard to know someone that well. People are surprising sometimes…"

"I know. But, I've known him awhile. He can be trusted."

"If so, then why isn't he here? How did I end up outside? Why can't I remember it…or him?" She swallowed hard, fighting the power of uncertainty. He gently cupped her face. "I don't know. But, I promise we'll figure it out…together. Okay?"

She nodded, suddenly drawn to his conviction and tender care. For a brief moment, it didn't matter who she had possibly been with that night. The young man before her seemed to be all that was important. She felt both intrigued and comforted by his presence. Then, it seemed her body was leaning toward him of its own volition. His gaze fell to her mouth and she began to tremble before he set his lips to hers. His kiss was a wonder not often spoke of, an exploration of certainty and passion. As she melted into his arms, she wondered why no one had described it to her before, the insistent thud of her heart or the warmth in her stomach, the way her fingers itched to touch or pull him closer. How could lips provide such comfort yet also a passage into a world she had not known before but yearned for now? How could a man be so careful as he was in his kiss, eager yet cautious as he explored her with lips and tongue? She had not heard of such a thing. Was it possible that this man, who seemed to consider her feelings in every way, could be trusted? When he pulled away, Justin appeared as spellbound as she felt. A short breath escaped him. "I, I'm sorry. I shouldn't have done that. You're already spoken for."

But, was she? She wasn't entirely sure that what was said about Saturday night was true. Perhaps he had been mistaken and it had really been the opposite. Maybe Justin's friend was only helping her, not showing an interest in her, or doing anything more. Either way, nothing was certain. And she had to know the truth before she could even decipher Justin's kiss.

****

Despite her need to unravel the events at the party, she couldn't stop thinking about what Justin had done that afternoon. She had never thought of herself as attractive. The fact that Justin had kissed her seemed unimaginable. She supposed she should be more concerned about what had happened the night of the frat party, but she couldn't help thinking that the kiss had meant something. Justin might have felt something for her and might still. She couldn't tell; she didn't know many men besides her father and even knowing him left her wondering if she knew how they ticked at all. The image of Justin's face and the sensation of his kiss never left her, neither that night nor the next day after she had returned home from her Latin class. A knock on the door woke her from the daydream. Her roommates wouldn't be back from class yet. Shrugging, Angelica slid off of her bed and, stepping over the piles of Karen's clothing in the freshman space, answered the door. On the other side was a tall, muscled guy with sand-colored hair and blue-gray eyes. He looked like a surfer straight out of an extreme sports network. "Yes?"

"Is Angelica around?"

Frowning, she tried to hide his view of her tattered lounging clothes. "That's me. Can I help you with something?"

"Justin sent me. He said you both were looking for me. I've been out of town to see my parents. I left early Sunday morning." He studied her expression for a moment. "You don't believe me."

She tried to appear nonchalant. "That's kind of sudden to take off just before classes. It's Wednesday."

"I know. But, I didn't plan it or anything."

"Oh? Family emergency?"

"You could say that."

She shifted uneasily. "I'm sorry. I didn't get your name." She dared not think this was the guy Justin had spoken of. Something just didn't fit with his story. Not to mention he was a complete stranger and she didn't consort with strange men; usually.

"Oh. Brendan Hammond." He shook her hand in an awkward manner.

"You're Brendan."

"Yes."

She cocked her head and sighed. "You didn't recognize me from before?"

"You'll have to forgive me. I'd had several drinks that night. And you looked different then, more makeup and all. You didn't tell me your name either."

"I see."

"You still don't believe me." He pulled out his wallet from the back pocket of his jeans and showed her his license.

Sure enough, the right name was printed on the card along with a good picture. "The fake I.D. business is getting hard to pin down these days."

His face lost its vibrancy. He suddenly appeared haggard, like a man who'd been in the coal mining business for far too long. Brendan cleared his throat. "I should be going."

"Wait!" She grasped his arm. "I'm sorry. That was a bad joke. I really need to brush up on my people skills."

He attempted a small smile. "It wasn't that bad." He sighed. "I'm no good with small talk-"

"Me neither."

"Do you want to take a walk?"

"Sure." Despite the fact that she was exiting the house in her oldest jeans and the most tattered t-shirt in her closet, they needed to talk. She locked up and followed Brendan down the dormitory hallway. When they were a good distance from the building and headed toward the quad, Angelica spoke to cover for the silence. "I'm glad you're really Brendan. I began to think you didn't exist. You see, I've been going kind of crazy about this whole thing."

"I heard."

"What?"

"Well, just that you didn't know what happened that night."

"That's right. I suppose you think I'm weak and I can't hold my alcohol. Well, I guess I can't. I don't drink usually. And I'm certainly not the partying kind."

"What were you doing there then?"

She had never really asked herself that question, though she had wondered about her own insanity afterwards. "I don't know. Perhaps it was to prove a point. The fact is that I ended up in the wrong place at the wrong time."

"It wasn't so wrong."

"What was right about it, Brendan? I woke up on the lawn with the worst headache of my life and then, there were people telling me I'd slept with a complete stranger. That's not like me at all."

He sighed. "We didn't do anything wrong. I can assure you of that."

Frustration rose to the surface. "You said you didn't remember everything."

He frowned. "I remember that."

She sighed, uncertain she could trust him. "Can you assure me that it was completely platonic?"

"Well, yes. We didn't do anything. I think we danced for a while-"

"You think? I don't even dance."

"Well, you did then. And we went upstairs to my room."

"And?"

"You seemed tired. So was I. We fell asleep, Angelica. Is there a crime in that?"

"I suppose not." She thought hard. "Is that it? That can't be all."

"We were drunk. I might have accidentally touched you while I was asleep, but I did nothing else. When I woke up, we were dressed and everything."

"And you just left?"

"My cell phone rang. My mom was panicking. She thought my stepfather was having a heart attack. I had to leave."

Concern touched her. "Is he all right?"

"Yes. I mean, he did have one, but they say it was mild. I stayed as long as I could."

Angelica sighed. "Okay. So how did I end up outside?"

"Downstairs was completely trashed. I couldn't leave you in the room. Everyone would assume the worst that I, Brendan, keeper of all promises and rare, but loyal boyfriend that I am, walked out on a woman. How very civil of me. So I did the least conspicuous thing."

"You tried to erase me."

"No, I didn't think they would put the two together. At least if you were outside, you wouldn't have to deal with the guys. They can be, well, guys sometimes. It's juvenile. Anyway, I didn't expect that Justin would find you. But, of course, our reliable and constant designated driver would see you on the lawn. It was stupid of me. I'm sorry."

"The grass thing was a little careless, I'll admit. But, you didn't do anything else to me. We didn't..."

"No, and I wouldn't-"

A thought struck her then. "Oh, I get it. Choose the least attractive woman in the room, do a pity dance with her, get her drunk and ditch her. So, that's how the game works."

"Are you crazy? You're gorgeous. And I wasn't playing you. I don't even know you. Don't you understand? I date women first, a long time, before I even consider sex. I mean, I think about it, but I don't know anything about you. I couldn't sleep with someone I just met. It doesn't mean I'm not attracted to you."

She laughed. "Are you for real? There are actually guys like that?"

"Yes."

"Wow. I thought all the gentlemen had left the country."

"No, we're just harder to find." He sighed. "So, you seem kind of introverted, very intellectual, and a little old-fashioned. I should really hook you up with Justin. He's a sucker for that kind."

"Oh really?"

"Yeah, he's one himself."

"Justin, an introvert? I didn't detect that at all."

"Sure, and immensely sarcastic like yourself. You'd be perfect for each other."

"Uh, thanks, but I shouldn't. I have classes right now."

Brendan shook his head. "Figures. You introverts are all the same, never willing to take a risk, even if it's really important."

"What's so important?"

"Love; It changes everything."

I take it you've been in love before."

"Not really. But, I dream about it. Don't you?"

She couldn't deny she'd thought about it or that she'd considered that she and Justin could be together someday. "Maybe. I think I'll handle Justin on my own. As long as I have your consent?"

"Sure, I have no hold on you."

"Thanks, Brendan."

He winked. "No problem."

****

Angelica was hiding behind a tree when Justin came out of the Science building two days later. She fell into step beside him. "It's a beautiful day, isn't it?"

He started for a second, catching his breath. "I didn't see you."

"I get that a lot. So?"

He blinked. "Oh, yeah. A perfect day for hiking."

"You're into the outdoors?"

"Yes. Aren't you?"

"Of course. Listen, someone told me it was a good time to take a risk. What do you say I tag along?"

"On what?"

"Your hiking trip."

"I'm sort of a loner."

"Yeah, me too. But, I decided I was getting tired of being alone. Aren't you?"

He nodded. "Is this the first time you've ever asked a guy out?"

She nodded. "How did I do?"

"Not bad, really. It was subtle, but pushy."

She felt deflated suddenly. "I came on too strong then."

"No! Not really. I mean, it worked for me."

She grinned at him, then looked down at her feet. "So…"

"So, what happened with Brendan?"

"Oh, that. There really was nothing there to begin with. It didn't work out. We were just too…"

"Different?"

"Exactly."

"I had a feeling he wasn't the one for you."

"Yeah, actually I had someone else in mind. I've only known him for a little while. But, somehow, without my knowing it before, we have so much in common. And sometimes we even finish each other's sentences."

"Who is this guy then? You just met him?"

"No, he actually saved me a few days ago. Found me passed out on some strange lawn, not knowing where I was or what I'd done. It was amazing...well, the part where I met him. He kind of changed my life. It's strange, but somehow he's a part of me now and I can't do anything to prevent it. It was an interesting experience. I'll have to tell you about it sometime."

Justin smiled and held her hand, but kept her from walking with another hand at her waist. "I suppose it all started with a kiss then?"

"No, but that helped. Plus a little compassion, comfort and-"

"Love?"

"Love? Well, that could happen. If it does, I won't try to stop it."

"You won't?"

"No. Why would I try to stop love? That's silly."

"It's been known to happen...out of fear."

"But, Justin, I'm not afraid anymore."

"Yeah, me neither." Gently, he lowered his lips to hers for a slow kiss.

Angelica giggled as he pulled her close. She hadn't felt this happy in a long time. Life was certainly changing. If love was part of that change, then she would welcome it. There was nothing left to lose.

Breathing Room

By Marie Lavender

Jamie sifted through the letters carefully. Each one was set a month apart, as if the timing had been planned perfectly. She read select phrases in the letters, trying to get a picture of where Brian was and the mindset he had been in when he'd written them. She could picture him at a long desk composing a letter while a secretary typed away in the next room. Jamie looked out the window, noting the perpetual sway of the trees in the wind and the way the waves crashed over the beach not far from the house. He had been gone for six months. Six months and eight days to be exact. And she was still waiting for him. The locals would ask her why she didn't socialize more. They invited her to various gatherings in an attempt to push her forward in the right direction. She did not want to be pushed. He was still writing to her; he still cared. His absence would be obvious as long as he did. She pushed away from the desk and headed down the hall to the kitchen. She opened the back door and went down to the beach. The season was changing quickly. She could tell. It was early in the day, but the brisk air caused her to pull her caftan more closely about her. She stared out into the expanse of the ocean, feeling a kind of emptiness settle inside her. It seemed she had been waiting her entire life for something spectacular, some life-altering event that might offer her a miracle. Her life had been mundane until she'd met Brian. Raised by two loving parents who supported her through anything, whether it was dating woes or a difficult term in school, she'd had a fairly normal existence. Her parents had supported her artistic avenues, but deep down she knew they wanted her to settle more than anything. It was the opinion that naturally restless people needed ties, even romantic ones, to help ground them Jamie never particularly understood this notion. She thought people set their own lives in motion that they had to go out and catch their dreams as if they were zookeepers bent on finding the rampant lion. Things did not just happen to Jamie. She was sure she had to do something drastic to change the course of her life. Living in a small town could do that to people. She wanted to seek every opportunity possible, every adventure. She needed to explore the world, to see what was beyond the limits of New Smyrna Beach, affectionately named "Smyrna". She knew it was how people figured out their places in life. When she met Brian, he represented all of those things. He'd moved to Smyrna from California, practically a world away. He was a military brat so he had seen all the places she longed to experience. And when she expressed this need, he would tell her about the big cities in America and Europe he'd spent time in. It was as if he felt by conveying his experiences; she would have no reason to want to go. And she didn't then. He was her center, the focus of her life. There was nothing else. She no longer needed her dreams. For some time, she was happy with her lot in life. Her parents had approved of him as a match and after some time passed; their feelings became strong for one another. She and Brian got married shortly thereafter and for a while, she lived contently with him while he finished his law degree. While he took classes, she painted. Then after he graduated, he'd decided to start a firm of his own rather than join a preexisting one. Smyrna was a quaint town as well. There wasn't much need for lawyers except for the occasional dispute between business owners or in cases like divorce. Brian commuted often to Orlando to look into what he would need to jump-start such a firm. Though Jamie's talents were sufficient enough to support herself, they were used to having more and soon she realized how much Brian would need to begin a law firm in Orlando. She took a job as a waitress at the Grille at Riverview, a well-to-do establishment that was perched over the water. The restaurant attracted many tourists because of the nearby spa. She painted when she could, but the demands of the house often kept her from doing so. That's when the fighting began. If it wasn't about money, it was about her sensitivity. If it had nothing to do with her faults, it had everything to do with his.

Now, it was different. Brian had left to ease the pain of their constant disagreements. Her art had always taken a second to his new law firm. Starting the firm required such a vast amount of money that it became the subject of discussion on most days. Their arguments had reached such a tumultuous level that neither could stand to be in the same room as the other. "Let's take a break", he had said and before she knew it, he had moved back to California to work near his grandfather, who was a judge there. It hadn't been in the cards...

Though she missed him, she was sure that part of the problem was the fact that she had never had the chance to figure out what she really wanted from her life. Some part of her resented him for that. Suppressing the urge to paint had become a constant need in light of the financial problems she and Brian were facing. Her work had ceased to be important. Jamie was sure it had to be now. Though she still waitressed, she would spend her days off creating ocean views, her specialty, or sometimes she would use her memories to construct a vivid scene from her childhood – the times she'd spent at her parents' house. Of course, she only had two or three days off per week to herself and that wasn't a whole lot of time to nurture her creative spark.

Her parents were often frustrated with her stubborn resistance of not accepting handouts. She'd had plenty of arguments with her parents recently about living alone. They wanted her to come back home, a two story giant in the heart of town where she'd lived before meeting Brian in college. Her refusal to be supported to that degree had caused several disagreements. They probably thought that Brian's absence would make her want to cling to those around her. It only made her want to do the opposite. She needed to feel worthy as an individual, to cope on her own. And their persistence made her feel as if she was being pulled in many different directions. She was tired of needing to please others. Her parents also wanted her to move on. Just last week, her mother had called to try to get her involved in another social function. "It's just a pool party, dear. Everyone will be there."

"Then I'm sure I won't be missed."

"Of course you will. Why, everyone keeps asking about you, why you stay shut up in that house all of the time." She sighed. "Did you tell them I actually work? Some of them have never lifted a finger in their lives."

***

"That's irrelevant, dear. They just want to be sure you're still alive and well. Oh, won't you come? It will be fun."

It will be duller than my sixteenth birthday party, she thought. She could imagine the questions too. How everyone would carefully jump around the subject of her separation with her husband, and why she wasn't looking for other prospects. Wouldn't tongues start flapping when they learned she was paying her own bills? She'd rather not deal with that kind of attention. "No, mother, I can't. I have to work that day."

"Will you come to dinner tonight then?"

Now, that she could handle. At least for an hour or two until her father, with his disconcerting frown and gentle blue eyes, asked her to take a check for her rent. And then, she would politely refuse before he became exasperated with her. Her parents had seemed to take her separation well though. She supposed they really wanted her to be happy and knew that whatever happened was for the best. But, every once in a while, her mother would gush about a new, single doctor she'd seen at the country club. It usually became an over-exaggerated form of propaganda, as if her mother was trying to sell her a bottle of perfume instead of sparking her interest in another human being. Jamie wasn't ready to start looking for other potentials. She still didn't know if Brian was even supposed to be a part of her life, but she did know that she couldn't let him back in until she was ready. So she was waiting...again. Jamie frowned. It angered her that being with Brian had somehow made her passive. No longer taking the initiative, she sought her chances in vain. Turning away from the beach, she headed back into the house through the back door. In the kitchen, she turned on the burner to heat water for tea. I should just go, she thought. *I should take off to Ireland or Tahiti and say to hell with waiting.* She could easily. She had just received a generous check from Mr. Thompson, a man who owned the Gagosian Gallery in New York City, another place she'd never been. But then what? What would she do once she saw those places? Would she return to Florida and forever spend her days in the midst of close-minded individuals? She didn't want that either. She didn't know what she wanted. She just needed to get out of Smyrna. Jamie switched off the burner and picked up the phone. "Yes, information, please. I need the number for the airport." As the call connected, she looked over at a picture that was hanging on the kitchen wall. She and Brian were running down the beach, laughing together. His nearly black hair was blowing in the wind. He looked as dashing as ever and she suddenly had an urge to run her fingers through his hair. She shook her head. His absence caused such urges. Jamie wished she could share this with him, but it was something she needed to do alone. With that in mind, she gave her destination to the woman on the phone.

****

Jamie stepped through the terminal and into the airport filled with lines of people and constant messages over a loud speaker. Along her nerves ran a strange euphoria as she lugged her carry-on bag over her left shoulder. The flight had not been so bad. She was surprised she'd actually braved the rough takeoffs and the turbulence the crew had experienced along the way to Madrid. She'd had faith that she was meant to take the trip and despite it being her first time, she knew everything would be okay. Her parents had advised her against taking the trip; they hadn't wanted her to go. Though everyone thought she should move away from her concentration on Brian, they had not meant it literally. The mindset was that all things were safer in Smyrna, even starting anew. She did not want to feel tied to that anymore. It had been three days since she had made the travel plans and now she was here. She had chosen Madrid because a week before, she'd watched a travel show about it and she remembered how she had thought it would be nice to experience it in person. Spontaneity was not always a bad thing. As she moved toward the airport's tall entrance doors, she felt a hand on her shoulder. Fear clutching her like a vise, she whirled toward the stranger behind her. A medium-sized man with olive skin cleared his throat. He spoke with a thick accent as if his throat was clogged with coffee grounds. "Excuse me, *señorita*. But, are you Jamie Reesen?"

"Why?"

"There is a phone call for you. There is a phone call for you."

"Oh. Where can I take it?"

"In the gift shop. There's a phone by the register."

"Thank you." She headed in the direction he gestured to and once she was in the midst of postcards and pictures of Spanish castles from centuries past, she found the phone. She frowned as she picked up the receiver. Not many people knew exactly where she was heading.

"Hello?"

"Jamie?" The baritone of his voice reverberated across the line.

"Brian..." It was too soon. She wasn't ready to talk to him yet. Swallowing hard, she held the phone closer to her ear.

"Look, I heard you were traveling. You should have called or written-"

"Why?"

"Because I know-"

"Why? So you can tell me I'm wasting my time with certain places? I'd like to discover that for myself."

"Yes, but Jamie-"

"Don't, Brian."

"I don't want to fight."

"I know." She sighed. "But, I don't need you telling me what I can or can't do."

"Jamie, I've never-"

"Stop it." She was very tempted to hang up without warning. He had that soft, defenseless tone now, and he knew that was her undoing. "Brian, wake up. We can't stop fighting. We separated for a reason." She could hear his defeated sigh on the other end. "I have to do this alone. Maybe someday you'll understand that. I'll call you when I get back, okay?"

"Yeah, okay. Enjoy yourself. I just wish..."

The desperation in his voice broke the fight in her. "What?"

"I wish you hadn't gone alone."

"I need to do this, Brian."

"I know. Jamie?"

"Yeah?"

"I'm sorry." She frowned. She knew he was talking about more than the phone call. "I know. I'll talk to you later. Bye." She hung up then, exhausted by the mixture of emotions he somehow had the power to cause. She groaned softly, frustrated that for those moments during the call, he had been trying to persuade her to return home and she'd felt she needed to justify herself to him. From the gift shop, she called for a taxi to take her to the Hotel Emperador. Perhaps then she could start to enjoy this trip.

****

Jamie discarded her luggage and the complimentary bag of toiletries the hotel employees had offered her upon her arrival. Inside, there was even a whole box of Spanish chocolates. How generous. Laying it all on a sofa, she crossed the suite and flopped her body onto the giving softness of the mattress overlaid with a dark red comforter. Jet lag, the blessed effects of a spontaneous flight made in the wee hours of the morning. Somehow she could vaguely remember a warning about the exhaustion that might overtake her after the pace of the trip slowed down. She shook her head, rolling over to get a good look at the clock on the nightstand beside the bed. Five o'clock. Normally she would be hungry by now, but due to the time difference, she would have to let her stomach grow accustomed to the new schedule. It was funny. Though her body was leaden with want of sleep, her mind spun a web of contrasting thoughts. She could only assume that there was a rat within the bond of trust she'd formed at Smyrna. Her parents had known of her departure as well as a few neighbors and friends. Therefore, someone had informed Brian that she was traveling. She had not contacted him in a while and had not planned to reply to his most recent letter until she returned from the trip.

Her parents might have told him. Even though they just wanted her to be happy, they surely could not know what she ultimately wanted – Brian or to be far away from Smyrna. She knew her mother had a soft spot for Brian's charm; she might have let it slip that Jamie was taking a trip to Madrid. And since he knew the exact airport and flight at which to contact her that made her suspect her family even more. It was good to know there was a little conspiracy against her. She knew who not to trust the next time she traveled. At least no one knew where she was staying in Madrid. The hotel staff had treated her well, considering what she had been prepared to expect. No one wanted a foreigner in his country. There was a resentment demonstrated with Americans especially, but she had yet to experience it firsthand. Part of it, she was sure, had to do with the language barrier. American dialects were so strange and the strong Spanish accents caused her some pause as well. The employees of the hotel had been accommodating however, ready with open arms and sincere smiles to fulfill her requests, even though she asked very little of them. She had not received any of the ill treatment the community of Smyrna had warned her about. The Spaniards could not be that bad, surely. But then, their genial behavior might be explained easily because Madrid experienced a current of tourism during specific months. Though many people in Smyrna preferred to stay there because of its familiarity, some of its newcomers would gossip about their trips through Europe and such. Madrid was just one of the many on that list due to its numerous sights like the Puente de Toledo, a bridge that lay over the Manzanares River, the renowned bull fights and the popular "Flamenco" dancers in the city. Jamie wanted to see everything on this trip. The people, the architecture…before it was over, she planned to be infected by the wonders of the city to a degree that she might never wish to return. She sighed. That was a dream, not a reality, to escape from the humdrum of her life in Smyrna. To remain anonymous, to go on unmissed. But, there would always be someone or something calling her back. She half-wished the connections she'd made with others had never occurred. It might be easier to let go if she made another hasty decision.

****

She awoke with hazy vision and limp muscles, mildly convinced that the Spanish chocolates had been secretly carrying a sedative. She shook off the effects of a dreamless sleep and headed into the bathroom where she saw in the mirror the wrinkles which contributed to her disheveled appearance – an uncombed mass of long, brown hair which fell into her hazel eyes. She had slept in her clothes. "Great," she muttered, still seeking guidance from any solid surface. Taking a long breath in, she decided that she would begin the day in style.

After a luxurious bath, she would don a bathrobe and have someone send up some scones – what did they eat in Spain anyway – for breakfast. Her belly was begging for sustenance and it had waited long enough. Once she pulled on the navy terry cloth robe and sat on the sofa, she sampled some of the finest hot chocolate she'd ever tasted and enjoyed a small plate of oddly shaped pastries. After breakfast, she dressed quickly and called for a taxi to begin her sightseeing. The driver, a man of medium stature and much curiosity about a female tourist, seemed pleased to give her a small tour as the car passed vistas such as the Prado Museum and the flea market, which was a popular attraction for tourists seeking their share of souvenirs. They also passed the Plaza Monumental where the bullfights were held, but the Spanish man advised her that the best day to see such a thing was Sunday. Throughout the drive, Jamie was practically glued to the window. The city was filled with life from the daylight that spilled over the tall buildings to the caravans of people who walked the streets of Madrid without a care in the world. It fit all of the descriptions she'd heard about New York City, but then it didn't. She knew that there, it was about survival of the fittest. In Madrid, she sensed the small town concern for one another while maintaining individual respect. On the streets, strangers spoke to strangers politely in passing, but were also willing to help when necessary. The place was commercialized, yet it still kept a slow pace. The only people who seemed to be rushing were the men and women in business attire, ready to face the next big task. Everyone else moved about the city with an ease of familiarity and a lack of concern for time constraints. At about midday, she was told, everyone partook in the *siesta*. During this time, all the citizens retreated indoors for a period of two to three hours. Time stopped and business stopped and it seemed that at the end of this *siesta*, everyone emerged from their houses refreshed and ready to continue with their daily errands. This gave Jamie some pause and she leaned forward to study the man's face. "Are you sure?"

"*Sí, Señorita*. It is customary."

She watched as he smiled a slow smile, possibly grinning at her naivety. "How long have you been doing this?"

"*Siglos*. Centuries. It is an old custom."

***

She sat back against the leather seat. *A customary time given for relaxation?* Surely the cab driver was kidding an American girl; it was his way of seeing how gullible she was. As soon as she was dropped off at the steps of the Prado Museum as requested since she was curious about the art of Spain, the sun beat hot over her head and she wished she had worn a skirt instead of jeans. It was then she noticed that no one was around. The streets were sparse and the square in front of the museum had been abandoned. The city that had been singing with life hours before had become a ghost town. The customary sounds of traffic and church bells were gone. There was only air and birds flying overhead. Complete stillness. Had everyone simply retreated inside to while away the hours when the sun was at its most intense? It seemed the taxi driver had been right. It was the time of the siesta. Time had slowed down to the point of nonexistence. No deadlines. No plans. Nothing mattered, but the stillness. Jamie, breathing the air slowly into her lungs, looked at the tall, ivory pillars of the Prado Museum. The architecture of it was magnificent. It was like a glorified version of a Greek temple if that was possible. She had an urge to capture it on canvas. She wondered if she could alter the light to emphasize its brilliance. Perhaps tomorrow she would find the perfect spot and pull out her brushes and paints, ready to start a new day. She felt inspired. She smiled slowly. Madrid was really something else. Why did Brian want to spoil the surprise for her? A place like this simply could not be missed or discarded on a whim. It called to the artist in her. And the customs spoke volumes to her. If people could voluntarily stop time, even if it was only a mutual agreement to remain inside for a few hours a day, then there was hope for humanity yet. If people just slowed down to think or reflect every once in a while they would probably be happier. At that moment, Jamie wanted to experience that custom with the rest of Spain. Seeing the unlikelihood of finding another cab driver on duty, she jogged across the square to a back entrance, which, she saw with the help of a sign, led into a train station.

She entered the revolving door, found a bench and rested there.

Her eyes to near slits, she spotted a row of telephone booths. Fighting a strong inclination to call Brian, she closed her eyes, throwing her arm above her head. Brian could wait. She had been waiting for six months, hadn't she? Jamie knew that this time, she would not miss out on Madrid. Or anything else for that matter.

Wash Day at the River
By Alfancena

The sound of the rooster woke her. Suzey slowly turned to look at the clock radio and it was 5:30 a.m. She didn't want to get out of bed, but she had no choice; it was wash day and she had to go to the river. There was no public water system in her town for homes. She liked going to the river early to wash before the sun got hot. Suzey liked to put the clothes out to dry and have some fun while the clothes dried.

Suzey had packed her dirty laundry in bags the night before. She also packaged light lunch/snack in case she stayed longer than planned. She got dressed, went to the kitchen to fix her a bowl of oatmeal. She liked having oatmeal because oatmeal lasted longer in her system, especially when she did not want to stop when she was on a roll with her washing. She added a yellow banana to her oatmeal, and she was very satisfied. She gathered her stuff, clothes, bar of detergent and wash brush. She rarely used a brush at the river because she mainly used the river stones for her brush. She had to load her goods in a cart because she could not carry all that by herself and the river was about a mile and a half from her home. The cart was made by her brother's own hands from scrap materials from old motor vehicles and wood. The wheels were made from old tires and nails. The body of the cart was about five feet long made from the board. The axles were made from two by fours. The steering wheel was from an old motor vehicle attached with strong plastic rope to the front wheels to drive the cart. It was equipped with brakes on the back wheels. Some were made without brakes; the drivers were very skillful in using their feet to stop the cart. Carts were used to transport all kind of goods or used for fun on afternoon joyride, especially on the weekend.

Suzey lived on a hill, so she always had fun steering her cart down the hill. Her hair whipped in the air, as she sailed downhill and the wind in her face was heavenly. The sky beyond the hills was orange red, which signified the sun was about to show its beautiful face. She knew that she would finish her washing before the sun got hot. She was not alone on the road, many farmers were heading to the fields; school children and adults were waiting for public transportation to start their daily event.

This was a very friendly town, so everyone greeted each other with a smile and words of encouragement. When she got to the river, she thought she would be alone, but it was wash day for others too. The ladies greeted each other and chatted a bit about family. The conversation almost ended abruptly as each lady walked away to their favorite spot to get their laundry done. The water was cool and felt so refreshing as Suzey waded in the river bed. She sat on her favorite rock, and started her first load of laundry. Suzey liked to hear the clothes flapped in the wind, so she traveled with rope for a clothesline. She tied the rope between two trees, and hanged her first set of clothes out to dry. She stopped for a minute, walked over to the Rose- apple tree and picked a couple of the fruit and sat down to eat.

By the time she was done with her second load of clothes, the first set was all dried. She took them from the line, folded them neatly, and placed them in her basket. Suzey liked doing that because she would not have to iron most of the pieces. The second set was hung on the line, so Suzey went to another part of the river which was much deeper and free of rocks and stones. She was joined by some of the ladies for a time of diving and swimming in the river.

There was much laughter and squeals of joy as the women tried new skills in their swimming technique and raced against each other. After frolicking in the river, the ladies sat down on the beautiful green grass to have their mid-morning snack. Suzey had one more load of clothes to wash, which she planned to do as soon as she was finished eating. And of course her second load was all dried and smelled so fresh. She folded her clothes and placed them in her basket. Now, with the sun getting higher in the sky, the river water felt warmer. Suzey got through her last load and hanged them out to dry. She found a very private area along the river, which was protected by trees and gave herself a bath. Bathing in the river on wash day was one of her rituals of that day. She planned to lie on the grass to relax and wait for her final load to dry. The load was much lighter to transport when the clothes were dry.

Suzey spread her blanket under the shade of the almond tree and before she knew it, she was fast asleep. She went into a deep sleep and of course she went to dreamland. She dreamt that she walked to the other side of the mountain by the river. She had never seen anything or place so beautiful. There were flowers of many hues in a very neat garden. There was a swing on a beautiful stone patio in the middle of the garden. She looked up from the garden and behold, there was a beautiful white long cabin with a baby blue door and shutters. She wondered who lived there and started up the path to the front door. On her way to the front door, she had to cross over on a small bridge. She stopped to look at the spring and it was the most fantastic spring water she had seen. The stones at the bottom of the spring, along with clear water looked like crystal. The sound of the water running over the rocks played a gleeful tune. She took a deep breath and said, "This place feels like heaven." At the end of the bridge there was a sign stating, 'CRYSTAL SPRING' she giggled to herself and said I am not the only one who saw the spring was like crystal. She made it to the front door and there was a sign on the door. She read the sign and she could not believe what she read, "Suzey, this house belongs to you, walk right in." She read it again. She looked around curiously. The windows were opened and pretty yellow and white curtains moved gently in the breeze. Although she was concerned, she was also curious to see what was inside. She turned the doorknob gently and was about to peer inside when she heard her name. She turned to look, mmm, mmm, she opened her eyes to see one of her friends standing over her. Her friend told her, that they were leaving and did not want to leave you alone sleeping. Suzey could not believe her adventure was only a dream. It took her a minute to get herself together. She thanked her friend for waking her and got her load of clothes from the line. She packed her stuff and headed home. Another wash day at the river ended, and until next time, she left the river behind.

Women of the Snow

By Phibby Venable

Yesterday on the beach
she was a sea gull
a seal heart
a short coat unbuttoned
and reading aloud
In the spring she read
a bridal magazine
chose house shoes
flung long soulful looks
into the large square
of the picture window
where golden rings tightened
around the drapery drawback
around her finger
around the crime scene
where the victim lay
But she had witnessed
women in the snow
in the tarot card
in an ice storm
in the restaurants of bad backs
and the faces of laurels
withering in the cold

The women in the snow
held empty bowls
and sturdy shoes they carried
in large bags
beside the sweet talk of a loser
They cultivated gray matter
and spoke like wood chopping
on a dull stump
Some of the women screamed
in the snow with children
They were in agony
they got their feet wet
they threw shrill vowels
when the children vomited
They stuck lost kisses
on apartment shelves
But the way she wanted out
was in a strong wind, on a reindeer,
in the back seat of Santa's sled
with a moisturizer and a manicure
and a mirror that held a light inside
She wanted five hundred feet
from ocean front
in a short coat,
unbuttoned,
with a seal heart and a sea gull
and a new start
in a palm tree with a sun beam
with a red flower
and a book sleeve
where she could read
or she could write
till her eyes fell
on a fairy tale
that she struck down
with a sea weed
then she read the part

in the gray print
where the brain lived
and she stayed there
till she grew up again
where the only rings
were around the sun
and around her head
when the hot breeze
and her hair flew
in the beggar wind.

By phibby

Morning Delight
By Dawn

Morning Delight

The stars have danced with the moon
For many an hour, until all are
Ready to call it a night.
A hush begins to spread across the sky.
Moon sighs, and drops below the horizon.
Stars fade as they roll over and cover up with sky.

Sun gently pulls herself higher and higher.
Sky softens to pink and then turns golden.
Ocean waves catch the first rays of new day.
Seagulls begin to awaken noisily.
Hunger makes them take flight.
Breakfast of sea creatures will soon be theirs.
Three white horses meander down from the hills.
On to the silky beach, they play in the waves.
Salt spray chases them as a race begins.
Sunlight sparkles like diamonds through the spray.
Legs churn among the waves gaining speed.
Steam from nostrils shows their determination. On and on, they race
playfully,
Nickering encouragement to the current straggler.
They pass on down the beach with tails flagging behind.
Hooves pound the beach in staccato fashion, and then fade.
What an enchanting sight to behold, this morn!
Sun smiles happily to beckon all to start their day.

2014 © Dawn L. Huffaker

Life Passes Her By

By Kathryn Chastain Treat

Life Passes Her By

She sits and stares out the window
and she doesn't recognize anything
Life has passed her by and
nothing is the same

Where was she when all this happened?
She was here but

Life passed her by
Buildings were built and
buildings were torn down
People arrived and left
People were born and others died
Life passed her by

People divorced and
others married
People found new jobs and
new hobbies
Where was she--she was
there by she did not participate
in life

It passed her by
She reaches out but
touches nothing
Life is just past
her grasp
She stretches and bends
and tries again
But life passes her by

She talks to people but
it is a jumble
to understand what they say
The life she missed is
just out of her reach
Life passed her by

Wolf Winds

By Phibby Venable

Wolf Winds

The air so soft and lavender
with wolf winds slipping through the trees
My aspects dance on stiffened limbs
Yesterday, at Pearl Head Creek,
a water laced with pure white stones,
I saw a mountain woman's face
She hunkered where the water ran
to gather in a gallon jug
enough of it to carry home
Her skin was lined, and Irish fair -
threads of red and white streaked hair
The eyes she lifted to my face
were calm, and clear, and full of light
But somewhere in the depths I saw
the blue of bruising often found
in those who have surrendered ground

She had the look I've often glimpsed
of grief grown calm and motionless
Yet still, the wide, evocative smile
of one who thinks of much to give

She did not say an unkind thing
simply remarked upon the stream
and how the water ran so clean
And running clean is what I thought
I think it often when I see
Tired hearts that walk with poverty
Crushed beauty in their once young lips
A different crushing in the eyes -
where long lost hopes have stepped aside
and still they smile, and still they smile

If Only

By Kathryn Chastain Treat

IF ONLY

Feeling all alone

no one wants to talk

The weather is bad

can't go for a walk

With friends there

is no common thread

Our conversations

are empty and dead

No new movies

have I seen

I feel like I have

the cooties and this is a bad dream

There seems to be

nothing to discuss

Talking and hearing about

me is too much fuss

My home is empty

and bare

A shell of a place

is all that is there

No comfy sofa, pillow,

or chairs to invite rest

Coffee, end tables, and

two dining chairs are what is left

In my home I feel

like a stranger

Because of this here

I do not want to linger

Will I ever feel

at home and at ease

In this cold house

with this awful disease

My life has been

turned upside down

I now wear less

smile and more frown

Meeting with friends

to talk an shop

All these fun things

have come to an end

To their homes for visits

I cannot go

I sit at home and

they do not show

Friendship with me

is now a bother and chore

Special soaps and clothes

before they come to my door

Less and less will

I hear from them

For Rick and I it will

just be me and him

I guess I can't

blame them for

I have really become

rather a bore

I haven't been here

or there

I really have nothing

to share

They saw a new movie

or found a new place to shop

I got a new food and

found a safe mop

We once had lots

in common to share

Our lives no longer

have anything to compare

I now feel sad

and lonely

and wonder

if only

If only I hadn't

chosen to work

Behind this mask

I would not lurk

If only I had not

developed this illness

I would not live in

so much stillness

If only I could

tolerate more

We could meet and

shop at the store

If only

Would I feel so lonely

<u>Your Kisses</u>

By Marie Lavender

I love your kisses.

I could write sonnets about your mouth,

the bow of your lips,

the power of those lips on mine, on my body.

I could write on and on because you have so many different
kisses.

You have a hello kiss,

the one you greet me with.

You have a goodbye kiss;

it's not a real goodbye kiss,

just a "hey, I'll see you in a few days but I really don't want to go" kiss.

You have a loving kiss;

I can feel your tenderness,

your affection for me in spades.

I close my eyes as your lips press to my brow or my cheek.

You have a gentleman kiss (I've always thought you were one).

With that kiss, I feel like the lady you've always said I was.

You kiss my hand or make a gesture that cements what I know about you,

a man of honor to the core.

You have a patient kiss too,

the kind where we feel unhurried.

I could drown in that kiss forever.

It is undemanding, yet still passionate somehow.

Then there is your sexy kiss,

the one that makes me breathless and hungry,

the one that amazes me as my body floods with feelings.

I can never get tired of it and yet it is novel each time,

as if a new facet of our love is added to the passion there.

Your sexy kiss drives me wild;

it makes me feel liberated too.

I can't name all the kisses in one sitting; there are too many,

so many to count.

So, I'll say you bless me with a different kind of kiss every day.

Oh, love,

I love you so very much.

And I love all of your kisses too.

All I Need

It was on a night like tonight that I lay,
wondering what it was I felt,
a kind of destiny taking form.
But, those lines were cast from the beginning, weren't they?
They stretched back centuries, way before we met,
in people we were before.
We have always been connected.
Our love is cosmic,
limitless.
That night, as I lay thinking about you,
a hearty ache inside of me, picturing you close to me,
I became more,
a being in love.
They say love makes you a fool.
Then I welcome foolishness,
for it's only my comfort with you that makes me dream bigger,
reach higher.
Nothing can break us.
No one can stop this force, this connection between us.
Miles away even, I think of you always.
I feel you beside me,
holding me close,
our hearts beating perfectly.

Though I miss you, I know all I have to do is think of you to know
you're no so far away.
You're my home. I'll always come back to you.
In mere days, I will see you again.

We will reunite,
my world will right itself.
Until then, I hold you close in my thoughts, as close as I can get,
just like you'd hold me.
I know one day soon,
times will get better,
a time when we can finally breathe as one.
I have a ring to prove your promise to me.
I have the look in your eyes when you say how much I mean to
you.
I've always trusted you to keep my heart safe.
I have these feelings inside,
this love that is beyond words, and it's enough.
And I'll wait.
I'll wait for that day when the world stops fighting us.
We're strong.
We've won every battle since the beginning.
You're mine, and I am yours.
That's really all that matters in this quiet night.
That's really all I need.

Four Wheels

By Dawn

Four Wheels

Four wheels roll to and fro.

Carry me from place to place.

Joystick steers the path they take.

An incredible machine is my wheelchair.

People don't often see the magic of my chair.

They see someone different than them.

Presume that I am not as capable as they.

Peg me as challenged and nothing more.

In school, it made me want to prove the teachers wrong.

Mom had always told me that there was no difference

Between me and other kids except that I couldn't walk.

Made me work extra hard at school studies to be the best.

Teachers soon learned that I was more than a wheelchair.

I took the lead in each class, and helped others with their studies.

Changed the label from being handicapped to an asset to them. They saw me for who I was and still am.

Graduated valedictorian from high school.

Graduated top of the class from college.

Founded a computer store and ran it for seventeen years.

Writing poetry for pleasure, for me, now.

Four wheels roll to and fro.

Carry me from place to place.

Joystick steers the path they take.

An incredible machine is my wheelchair - my legs.

By Marie Lavender

You're so close now it feels like you're a part of me.
Our breaths mingle,
Your fingertips flutter over my skin and my body tingles.
I can feel the reverence in your words and your touch.
I've never felt this way with anyone.
Time ceases as we lay here, skin to skin, breath to breath…
And I feel so fortunate to have found you so long ago.
Or maybe you found me.
In truth, you saved me.
Maybe I could have stood the loneliness, but could my soul have
taken the rest?
You made me believe in true love again. You prove it to me every
day.
You made me want to trust instead of live with my hurt, my
doubts, my cynicism.
You woke this girl up to love, not to an ideal, but to real love…

The kind of love that sees weakness as human, even as strength.
The kind of love that accepts weirdness.

The kind of love that takes secrets, hopes and dreams, and keeps
them safe.
The kind that stands the test of so many trials in life.
The unconditional kind.
Your hazel eyes steady me.
Your humor keeps me from taking myself too seriously.
I don't know where I'd be if I couldn't look at your face here
next to me or even across
the room,
If I couldn't look forward to the moment I walk down that aisle
towards you.
I think I'd be lost if I didn't have you.
I might survive.
My heart would still beat.
But, it's my soul you saved by appearing in my life.
It's the love I feel unfailingly that you've inspired.

You are my life, my purpose, my heart.
Fate brought us together,
But it's you I should thank.
My lover,
My savior.

HE WHO WOOS YOU LIKE NO MAN - a poem by Deepak Menon

Smoke swirled around your figure

Swaying like a misty wraith

Amongst the nameless crowd of souls

Dancing their Dance of Faith

Faith in the future they believed in

The future born in the dim past

When fought they battles, couldn't win,

And were into Destiny's Cauldron cast,

To flutter like trembling leaves in the wind

Frantically dancing the Dance they made

A Dance they made, *to make them forget*

The games of love they once had played

When into their midst, your timeless shape

Had burst in like a flash of light

Banishing the shadows, the smoke and dark

Scattering all fear into headlong flight

And you danced the ***Dance of Hope***

While stars sparkled in your lovely eyes

And your body sang a Song of Hope

Stilling the multitudes hopeless cries

And they watched with riveted gaze

Your swirling limbs, your haunting face

Your radiant smile, your tossing hair

Your twinkling feet in frantic race,

And they knew you danced for me

They watched and wondered frozen in time

While your eyes saw only me

Radiating your love - true, sublime

And they knew that they had seen

Eternity in your sparkling dance

A love so true, so pure - so strong

It left them speechless and askance!

And from the mist there appeared

I, who wooed you like no man!

Took form, and swept you far away

Into the Forever Sunshine land!

The Rapture

By Charles Ray

Sitting on the front porch

Watching the sun go down.

The pink glow against

The low hanging clouds.

Sipping too sweet tea

So cold it hurts my teeth,

And listening to the evening

Song of the frogs in the

Swamp, and the chirp

Of the crickets as they

Say farewell to the

Day. It just doesn't get

Any better than this.

By Peter Cacciolfi

When the aging lady went to the hardware store to purchase items for her garden, she had no idea what was going to happen to the inner structure of her back yard world. Emily was a kind lady who always had other people's best interests at heart. When visitors passed through her house, by special invitation only, they were led out into the garden to feast their eyes on the marvel of the miniature world. There were flowers unknown to the average person because Emily was gifted with a special ability to graft one plant into another, over and over again, until she was satisfied that the results of her efforts had produced a new species of garden life. Emily did this with all of the living things in her garden paradise. It was so successful and well known that it attracted requests for viewing everywhere. As every viewer left in awe at the vastness and variety of never before seen plants, no one ever looked closely at the micro-world, that place at ground level where species were measured in millimeters rather than inches. In fact, Emily had created a war zone oblivious to the viewing world because most everything was too small to see.

On this one particular day when a beautiful fairy was shaken from her haunt and thrust to the ground that the creatures decided enough was enough. The strongest leaders, including the fairy community, summoned a meeting of all creatures, big and small. A forum was held and there was a chairman who heard complaints from the attendees. The Hummingbirds complained because they couldn't feed on too many of the flowers because they didn't know how to approach them, so they were mostly frustrated. The squirrels and chipmunks complained because, although there were ample nuts from the trees and on the ground, they didn't know how to crack them open. Even the blue-jay and mighty crow couldn't crack the code (no pun). With the wealth of food to eat, most was wasted because little or nothing was known about the varieties or their values. Anarchy was close at hand. There was even talk of abandoning the area for gardens more familiar to the ground and tree dwellers. Rabbits couldn't decide which green leaves they should eat because there was talk about toxins, mostly idle rumors however. They began to lose weight. The birds could land anywhere, but when it was time for turning in for the evening, they weren't sure which tree shelters offered the safest protection from the elements and the night stalkers. The fairies, who had the knowledge from the past on their side were just as confused as the rest of the dwellers. They could flit and fly, but often they would bump into leaves that appeared to be light and fluffy only to find them stiff and hard. It was very difficult to observe a beautiful fairy bump her head and tumble to the ground, injured and confused.

Everyone loved Emily for the bountiful surroundings, but beyond all that, this kind old lady had created a monster of beauty. Beauty for the onlooker and a monster for those forced to try to navigate the maze of different, unknown roots and byways. Does a squirrel live in a hole in a tree that is hard on the outside, but sticky and gooey on the inside? I should say not. Does a bird find an abandoned hole in the trunk thinking it is safe to build her nest and raise her family only to find out that it fills with water, mysteriously? The flying species called it not for the birds. Where then were they to live without being threatened by the very structures that are supposed to provide shelter?

The day came when the final meeting was held. There were animals of every species, some rarely seen in public because they were given the "shy" gene, but they had to be heard. They all were at their wits end. The fairy in charge heard all complaints and made note of them, leaving no one out, because that wouldn't be fair. Then they took a vote on what was to be done.

After extensive brainstorming a brilliant, beautiful, dressed in pure white fairy appeared. Her sparkling wings resonated with the beauty of diamonds reflecting off the sun.

"Don't be alarmed, for your complaints have been heard far and wide, and I have been assigned to assist you in your quest to restore your lives back to normal. I was told to report to you that way out in an unknown location lives the Wizard of Wizards. He is famous for helping out humans who go astray or are abused and deprived of their rights. He has consented to hear your story and decide whether or not he would lend his magical talents to resolve this most traumatic situation without bringing in the Union of the animal and plant kingdom. The Wizard was summoned, and after many hours of reading notes and secret observations, he decided that he would venture out into a world not usually in his realm. He would try to capture the attention of Emily, without scaring her half to death, and explaining the dire conditions and situations she has unknowingly caused. How to meet Emily was going to be difficult. He went back to his Council and summoned a meeting for ideas. It was decided that a normal person in the form of a pretty young lady would approach Emily and explain who she is and what she is doing there. But most importantly, she had to get across the key to the problem, that being a willingness to meet with the Wizard without becoming too frightened. Emily had never heard of the Wizard, and wasn't familiar with the miniature world of life in her garden. Upon hearing just briefly what was happening she was heartbroken.

"Will the Wizard scare me?" she asked.

"No!" replied the pretty girl. "He is like us, but dresses differently and has a long beard. And although he possesses powerful magic, he only uses it for good against evil."

"Then I shall meet with him," announced Emily.

That being done, the Wizard of Wizardry swung into action and arranged for a meeting in the garden. He alerted all the creatures, great and small, of the meeting so that they would all be in attendance. When the Wizard saw the garden, he was awe-struck and couldn't believe his eyes. Never in his long career had he ever seen anything so beautiful and different. Different was the key word, for therein lay the problem. As the two adults met, the Wizard performed a few magical tricks which allowed Emily to observe the inner workings of the sub world with which she was not familiar. The more she saw the sadder she became. For the first time in her life she actually got to visit with her garden fairies. They explained, along with the Wizard, their plight and sadness. They assured Emily that they didn't want to abandon the garden because they were happy with her, but the confusion about all the strange and unknown plants was creating chaos amongst the creatures. Emily began to cry and was immediately comforted by the Wizard and the fairies. She didn't know what to do about the garden because she didn't know how to change things nicely back to the great way they were.

"Emily, please leave everything to me, for I have the power within to correct all bad situations and make them good. You need only to get a good night's sleep without worry, and in the morning I promise all will be good for all concerned.." With those words, he and the fairies vanished from the scene leaving Emily to her thoughts. In her sadness she retreated to her room, had her supper, and turned in for the night. In her sleep, Emily had the strangest dream. She dreamed that she had created the most unusual garden the world had ever known, and that she would be famous. She thrived in her glory and was proud of her creations. Upon awakening the following morning, Emily hurriedly dressed and darted out to her garden. She was sad to see that nothing was unusual about the surroundings, and that all her plants and trees were as they always were. As she looked around, she swore she saw a small creature with wings darting back and forth some distance from her. She passed it off as poor eyesight and went on with her business of maintaining her beautiful garden.

US

PnP Authors the writers who be
Write wonderful stories for everyone to see
It started out with just WE two
When Pattimari got through it grew and grew
And now we have such wonderful friends
Who search through the sites writing odds and ends

And now a book we '6' did write
Fraught with mystery, suspense and fright
Such wonderful people have joined our clan
Everyone always willing to help when they can
It's fiction and non, biography too
It's the type of story that suits you
We thank you each and every one
For helping to make this group such fun

Copyright by Peter Cacciolfi

By Pattimari

There once was a funny little hummingbird whose name was Dandies. He lived in the Hills of the Dandelions Fields with his other hummingbird friends. He was like no other hummingbird. For one thing, he was born with dandelions decorating the top of his head. All the other birds giggled at him, but he wasn't offended because he was a happy hummingbird who flew from flower to flower making whirring sounds with yellow dandelions decorating his head. He loved to fly and land in trees while he watched all of nature's things. Even with his unusual dandelion head, he was a beautiful hummingbird with bright colors of red and purple wings.

One day he dipped his long, slender beak into the cool water of the hill's pond to take in a drink of water, but instead sucked up a worm. Wouldn't you know it - it got stuck in his throat? He twisted and turned his head and it still wouldn't come out, the worm just wiggled. He went from tree to tree throwing his head to the right and then to the left. He did this all day and into the night.

Then along came a beautiful pink butterfly with tiny spots of blue and yellow whose name was Amethyst. Amethyst flew around flowers like a princess. She saw Dandies sitting on a limb and asked, "What in the world is wrong Dandies?" But all poor Dandies could do was slope his head from one side to the other.

Slope. Slope. Slope.

Finally out came the words and he said, "I have a worm stuck in my throat." Princess Amethyst Butterfly thought for a moment and then said, "Dandies, I know a Guardian over at the Special Garden of Seemore. Her name is Konswa. I am sure she will be able to help you. She always helps anyone who is in a gridlock."

Dandies Hummingbird was very happy to hear someone could help him with his horrible problem.

"Come on Dandies, follow me," said Amethyst as she flew off in the direction of the garden. They flew down the path along Blue Bell Shells and Daffodils, then over Poppy tails and fox tails, down by the river and across the bridge. They came across Sagger Snake who was sitting alone on a rock looking sad. Princess Amethyst Butterfly asked, "What's wrong Sagger Snake?"

Sagger Snake said, "I have lost my tail and I don't know what to do." Princess Amethyst Butterfly said, "Sagger Snake come with Dandies Hummingbird and me to see Destiny, the Guardian. She might be able to find your tail."

Sagger Snake lighted up like a light bulb.

So off the three went; down the path into the fields leading to Destiny. They came upon an intersection where they could go in four different directions. All three stood wondering which way to go. Princess Amethyst Butterfly said, "Oh dear, which way should we go?" All Dandies Hummingbird could do was slope and slope and slope his head. Sagger Snake said, "Without my tail I can't decide which direction to go"

They looked to the right, then to the left. All three shook their heads in bafflement.

All of a sudden Deagan Horse and his cousin Jordan Horse galloped over to Princess Amethyst Butterfly. Deagan Horse said, "I always go to the right when I don't know which way to go."

"If you go straight, you will reach a dry desert and nothing grows there. No one goes to the desert," said Jordan Horse.

Dandies Hummingbird took a closer look in all four directions and said, "I'm mighty confused, but we have to take a chance or we'll never make it to Konswa, the Guardian."

Princess Amethyst thanked Deagan Horse and Ryan Horse, and decided they should go to the left. She believed it was the right direction to go in order to get to Konswa, the Guardian.

A forceful voice said, "No! Go to the right because it's a shortcut. It is the right way to Konswa, the Guardian."

"Who said that? Sagger Snake cried out.

"Why, it's me. I'm Tony Rock."

All three turned their heads and looked at an old brown pile of rocks and saw the biggest unsightly rock pointing to the right.

"I do declare," said Dandies Hummingbird and then hurried off to the right. The other two followed. The three began their journey, walking down the path where wild flowers twinkled with their array of colors. They talked as they walked, about the Valley of the Yellow Stones.

Sagger Snake said, "Did you know that in the land of the ancients there was a place called the Valley of the Yellow Stones.

"Yes," said Dandies Hummingbird. "It was called that because of all the yellow stones in the great rivers and lakes where ancient people made beautiful jewelry and coins with the stones."

The three continued on down the path leading to Konswa. The clouds in the sky looked like white fluffy cotton balls and the hills were sprinkled with carpets of colored wild flowers. As the three walked along the side of the path, they came upon a big old tree with brown mushrooms growing by a smooth large rock.

They heard a deep voice say, "Tony Rock told you to take a short cut to the right, well, he was wrong. You should have gone with your first thought, Princess Amethyst Butterfly because going to the left was right. Remember to always believe in yourself. Tony Rock is a dreadful rock. He leads strangers to the bad land so spiders can have a feast when they wake up from their winter naps."

"I do declare," said Dandies Hummingbird.

"Oh, we were just about to cross over the Rosetta River. Who are you?" Princess Amethyst Butterfly called out.

"I'm Jimmy Mushroom. No, you must not cross over the Rosetta River. The sky gets dark and the trees start to move. They are alive and will surely destroy you long before you reach Konswa, the Guardian. Go down that embankment and you will reach a river; follow it and it will lead you to Konswa."

"Thank you, Jimmy Mushroom. You have saved our lives. How can we repay you for your kind warnings?" Princess Amethyst Butterfly asked.

"You may repay me by trusting in yourself." Jimmy Mushroom said, and then he turned and went back beside the tree.

"When I get my spots back, I shall always trust in myself," Sagger

Snake said.

Dandies Hummingbird started to thank Jimmy Mushroom, but all he could say was, "Hiccup. Hiccup. Hiccup."

The trees were watching as Jimmy Mushroom warned the three. They were swaying back and forth saying, "Don't go the way Tony Rock said to go."

Sagger Snake rolled down the hill while Dandies Hummingbird and Princess Amethyst Butterfly flew over the beauty of the valley.

"Oh, this is great fun!" Sagger Snake cried out as he rolled over grassy land and then into the sand near the river. Right away, all three saw a clearing on the other side of the river, and then saw a big tall gate.

"I see a garden gate!" Dandies Hummingbird squealed.

"I see a garden gate too! Sagger Snake yelled.

Princess Amethyst Butterfly flew over to the raft and hollered, "Hurry Sagger Snake. Hurry! Climb on the raft."

Soon after arriving and getting off the raft, all three stood wondering what to do as they looked at the huge white gate with tall stones and a large brass ring over the center of the gate. Dandies Hummingbird grabbed the ring with his beak and then dropped it. The door made a creaking sound and then slowly moved open. There stood a beautiful lady with a long, white dress made of daisies. She was stunning with her long, shiny glowing hair with glittering stars.

She stood proud and tall, holding onto a tall wooden staff with a crystal sphere on top and attached was an eagle's feather. Her eyes sparkled with kindness and beside her sat a golden brown lion with a fluffy yellow mane. Destiny stepped forward and said, "I'm Konswa, gate keeper of the Secret Garden of Cyrus, and this is Akish my lion guard of the garden."

Destiny smiled as she pointed her sphere at the gate and it opened wider. "You may enter the garden of Cyrus if you have a pure heart. Destiny pointed her crystal sphere toward the three and rays of light beamed with beautiful rainbow colors which swirled around them and quickly disappeared.

Konswa's smile was glowing as she put out her hand for them to come inside.

"All three of you have a pure heart; please enter into my garden."
As Soon as they entered the gate closed. Destiny Guardian asked them to follow her. She took them into a room overflowing with flowers and fruit trees of all kinds with soft, fluffy pillows of yellow, orange and red. Destiny sat down on her white pillow and pointed for them to join her on the colorful pillows. After each sat down, she asked them what she could do for them. Amethyst Butterfly began telling Destinyabout Dandies Hummingbird and how he has hiccups because he sucked up a worm and it stuck in his throat. Destiny immediately picked up one mint leaf off the table in front of her and then a eucalyptus leaf and put them into a glass. She stepped over to the spring water flowing in naturally from a stream coming in from the bed of rocks leading to the forest, and added water into the glass. She then squeezed nectar from the trumpet flower into the glass and handed it to Dandies Hummingbird.

"Dandies Hummingbird, you drink this and after you swallow the last drop say, *come out worm.*"

Dandies Hummingbird drank the last drop and then said, "Come out worm." Before he could hand the glass back to Konswa, he let out a big burp, then another burp. They were so forceful that the worm popped out.

"Oh, DestinyGuardian, thank you so much." Just as he started to say thank you again, another big burp come out and everybody laughed.

Sagger Snake stood up and said, "Konswa, I've lost all my spots. Can you help me?"

DestinyGuardian stepped over to the pond and dipped her hand into the bottom and drew out a hand full of clay mud and mixed it with a lotus flower and rubbed it all over Sagger Snake's back and then said, "Now, Sagger Snake, say, *I want my spots back.*"

After seeing how Destiny helped Dandies Butterfly, he cried out loudly, "I want my spots back!" Soon after, Princess Amethyst Butterfly screamed, "Look Sagger Snake, a spot appeared on your back. Oh look, another one!"

Sagger Snake squealed with joy and quickly thanked DestinyGuardian. Destiny beamed and then said, "I'm glad you all feel better my friends. Please allow me to show you my garden."

As she walked in the garden showing her new friends the beauty of nature, she told them that the garden was grown in ancient times where Kings and Queens used to walk through the gardens. Flowers used to sing while lush grass full of life swayed to the music. The music from the flowers was so magical that rainbows appeared so they could listen.

"See that waterfall? Destiny asked. "Tundra the unicorn who is the master of all the unicorns, used to bath in this waterfall."

As the four of them walked through the garden there were butterflies, snails, toads, frogs and hummingbirds of many colors and even hummingbirds with funny haircuts like Dandies. All were happy. Sagger Snake cried out, "I'd love to live here. It's the most beautiful place ever!"

"You are all welcome to stay if you would like." Destiny said in her silky voice.

Akish Lion roared his wishes, "Please stay you will be happy and safe here."

Sagger Snake cried out that he wanted to stay, and so did

Dandies Hummingbird as he flew around circles.

Princess Amethyst Butterfly said, "I must go back and fly the forest in search of those in need, but I will come back from time to time to see you all my friends."

"Oh please do." Akish Lion roared. "The more the merrier!"

They all sang songs of joy, dancing into the night and when Princess Amethyst Butterfly left the next morning, Dandies Hummingbird, Sagger Snake, DestinyGuardian, and Akish Lion were at the gate waving good-bye.

"Please come back soon Princess Amethyst Butterfly," they all called out in unison.

By Pattimari Sheets Cacciolfi

Peter & Pattimari Cacciolfi, husband and wife team writers are owners of PnPAuthors Promotions & PnPAuthorsPromotional Magazine. They have fun inviting PnPAuthors to join in on some of their books and then they publish them. All of the above authors are members of PnPAuthors and we are proud to have them with us.

Peter & Pattimari would like to thank Kathryn Treat for all her wonderful but hard work on getting this book proofed and published. Without her it would have been weeks before it was done. Thank you Kathryn!

God Helped Me

There are times when fools like I forget
God started sun to rise and let it set
Smoothed out what was my thick skin
And into my life let His love in.

God helped me write poems smoothly flowing
And always in right direction I am going
And after all my poems He had inspected
Gave Him credit for being produced and directed.

After writing more poems with much zeal
Before God I again will continue to kneel
Gave Him all my thanks along with praise
For His great grace which will truly amaze.

James Thomas Horn
Retired Veteran

James Horn said to me the other day, "Pattimari, how could anyone possibly appreciate all of my humor?" He also told me that I would never run into another poet anywhere similar to him.

I believe you Jim. You are unique. You are good. You are indeed a poet!

My Introductory Poem
I will write my sweet poems by the score
Also in addition maybe many more
And don't exactly like to brag or boast
But which ones do you like the most?
Each poem seems fine and smoothly flowing
When you get one, on you start growing
As you absorb them in your mind while reading
Which one was best either last or succeeding?
Mix my poems up after throwing in big bag
Which will be many causing it sometimes to sag
Poem leaping out and landing on the floor
Will be the one you always love and adore.

James Thomas Horn
Retired Veteran

A Whole Meal

What was it up to you were leading?
In world many people we must be feeding
And across our borders they keep coming
Walking on feet with no wheels that are humming.

Many are quite quiet and also maybe mute
If they could only have one piece of fruit
Or bread if it happens to be a heel
It could serve as a complete meal.

Along a path they all were wandering
New direction to go to had been pondering
God, we want you to be with us please
So amount of our food will start to increase.

James Thomas Horn
Retired Veteran

Inner Peace

So by devil will ever be infested
When God's words you have digested
To take you on a path straight and narrow
Which is often traveled by a small sparrow.

Make God your guide and on Him rely
And as days and time go passing by
An hour would be nice or at least a minute
To allow God to always come in it.

Say a prayer and truly thankful be
Allow God to destroy all of the debris
As your long life continues to increase
He will award you with inner peace.

James Thomas Horn
Retired Veteran

Author: Marlowe Sr. -Author of <u>Phantasy</u>

When My Father Died

We stood mute through the entire process, as if not just our bodies but even souls were submerged in utter grief. He did nothing for us; we've got no reason to feel anything for him. All through his life he cared only for himself and those other folks who'd also attended the funeral - most of them strangers to me. On the contrary, my gut feeling was that mom was probably relieved that a baggage was gone from her shoulders - after all, it was she who used to handle the family finances and saying that it was not difficult for her would be a lie. However, when you are in an arena of mourning and you don't want to mourn, you're at least expected to show a pretension of grief for reasons of etiquette. The open ground before us was parched at several places - there was no life form or flora around - just billows and billows of smoke. All that could be seen was a group of pyres with burning cadavers. Among the crowd there was a guy from the South, Mr. Zant; he was a friend of one of my father's friends. My father had invited him on a city tour here, before the unfortunate thing happened. I could well imagine how he might be feeling.

"How the hell did all this happen?" he asked me, unexpectedly, as we were about to enter our apartment. It was dusk at the time.

"Heart attack. Last night." Later on I wondered if I was being unnecessarily curt with him, but then again, I was not feeling that great myself and was therefore in no mood for conversation, especially with someone I had known only for twenty-four hours. Mom remained silent through the entire night. She said nothing to me except that my father had left me some business contracts and that I should look them up. Despite my outward 'devil-may-care' type of attitude, I was feeling a little worn out inside; so I thought that I should take a few days off and that those contracts could wait.

"I know that it is an improper time to say this but," Mr. Zant started in a hesitating manner, "I'm sorry about your father, but you know, the real reason why I am here is...

" I interrupted him, saying "Yeah, he'd invited you to a city tour? I know. Later. You can stay here until then." My mother had added more salt in the food that night than she'd normally. I figured it must be her tension; thankfully our guest didn't complain.

It was 10 pm. I turned off the lights in all the rooms in our apartment, including the kitchen. Our guest was going to sleep in the other room where we had a single bed, while mom and I slept in our bedroom as usual. Half-an hour later, I heard our guest snoring heavily, as a result of which, I couldn't sleep. A while later I heard the sound of clattering of utensils coming from our kitchen.

At first I felt a little petrified but a little later I mustered enough courage to shout "WHO IS IT?" with a little shudder still apparent in my voice. Soon enough, the clattering stopped.   Mom was woken up by my shout, "What is it?" she yawned, "Don't shout at night. Let me sleep..."

"Didn't you hear ANYTHING?"

"What?"

"Well...someone is making noises in our kitchen, that's WHAT."

"Don't be silly. There is no one in the kitchen. Mr. Zant is sleeping too."

The clattering of utensils was heard again.

"See?"

Mom mumbled "Could be some wind blowing" but I didn't believe her, for there was certainly no heavy wind blowing outside. All of a sudden, the sound of clattering stopped again.

About an hour later, I heard a familiar voice - my father's. It said, "Hey, you people are sleeping so peacefully here eh? I can't get sleep in that upper story. I can't, so I came down here. I want to sleep here."

I shook up a little at hearing the oh-so-familiar voice at an odd time.

"He used to love cooking. He'd spend a lot of time in the kitchen, with those utensils..." my mother commented casually. I found comment rather unexpected.

I got out of my bed and tried to turn on the lights. I could not believe that Mom was being cool about the whole thing. Maybe she was so tired that she didn't care. Maybe my father's death had taken a more serious toll on her health than I could imagine. Just then, a cold hand grabbed my wrist and said "No, not that one Son. Don't do it." even as I shrieked. I was too shocked to even raise my head up in order to get a full view of the figure; I was more interested in turning on the lights so as to make the figure - whoever it was - go away. The next moment, there was total silence in the room. I attempted to turn on the lights again and this time, I did it. I heaved a little. Then I saw a figure resembling the stature of my father, white as mist, fleeing from my room and then vanishing through the wall - all within a couple of seconds.

I then told my mother that I can't sleep any more in darkness. She agreed. I wasn't sure if it was an apparition of my father or not but it didn't matter. As a matter of fact, I never had much belief in ghosts, but circumstances were slowly driving me toward expecting the worst.

The next day, I woke up at 7am. It was winter and the sunshine was yet to enter our home. The lights had been on since last night and when I woke up I figured that I should leave them as is. I headed for the bathroom to relieve myself, whereupon I discovered that my father's tobacco pot was gone from the bathroom's shelf! Brushing his teeth with tobacco was one of his addictions and he used to keep the tobacco pot on that shelf. I didn't tell my mother about it, because I was afraid that she might freak out this time; moreover, I didn't want to disturb her sleep.

As I was done with my dirty work, I saw that Mom had woken up too. "Why do you keep the lights burning even in the day? Who do you think would pay the bill for this extra consumption huh? Better turn them off NOW." I was not quite ready to heed my mother after what'd happened last night so I said, "What if that odd figure visits us again? That's why I thought I should keep the lights on until the sunshine enters our home."

"Sun will rise soon - in just half-an hour maybe. Don't give too much emphasis on what happened last night okay? That odd figure might have simply emanated from your imagination. I suppose the stress of your father's death affected all of us. It was not real. I don't...I don't think you'd encounter it again. It is best not to get ourselves bothered by it. These things do happen to some people who lose their loved ones."

"Oh well," I took a long breath, "It better be as you say. I'm afraid I might have a heart attack too the next time I encounter it. By the way, shall I wake Mr. Zant up? He is still snoring loudly you see."

"I'd leave him to himself. Maybe he needs sleep more than us; he's just arrived from such a distant place and then, what was not to happen happened. You can well imagine the level of grief his mind must be engulfed in since then."

As we were talking in the partially-dark room, the same mist-like figure - then only his head and neck being visible - appeared, bowing before my mom, and said, "Shall I bring you the fish today?" The figure was holding my father's tobacco pot in his right hand while his left hand's index finger was red with tobacco. A chill ran down my spine. I remembered how my father had this habit of brushing teeth with his tobacco paste early in the morning.

Even after recognizing his voice, my mom didn't freak out as I had expected. Instead, with great composure, she said, "Look, it's not like it used to be, Hon, not any more. Don't you get it? You are dead now, a ghost. You can't live here anymore with us. Go away from our house, and don't come here again."

The figure vanished even as mom said, again casually, "He loved bringing me my favorite fish every day at this same time, even though he'd have none of it himself" and broke down. She later proposed that there was no need to keep the kitchen light burning too, even when we were done with our cooking.

For the next few days we continued to hear the sound of the clattering of utensils coming from our kitchen every time we went to bed at night. One night Mr. Zant asked us, "Do you have a lot of vermin in here?"

"Vermin? Why?"

"Every time I sleep at night I hear that same sound of utensils clattering - the sound is sometimes more jarring than other times. What is going ON here?"

I couldn't explain the inexplicable to him; I was worried he might make a scene and wake up the entire neighborhood, so I resorted to lies, "Yes, indeed we have a lot of rats in here."

"Why don't you get a mousetrap then and..."

"Because we DON'T want to, okay?" he was getting more irritating to me than even that annoying mist-like figure. "Why, does it bother you?"

He went off to his room and from what I heard, slumped on his bed.

One morning my mother became quite concerned about the whole thing and told me to arrange for a shradh for my dead father, as it might offer peace to his troubled soul and the ghost might stop visiting us again.

Mr. Zant who'd just woken up, asked her curiously, "What is a shradh, Aunt?"

"It's a food offering ceremony undertaken by the survivors of the deceased in order to pay their respects to the soul of the deceased."

"Oh, I see. If you don't mind, I'd like to know more about it, how it is performed, etc."

"Well, among other things, feeding the Hindu Brahmins is a must. It is said that only after the shradh is duly completed does the soul of the deceased find a place in heaven, with the Lord - in complete peace and harmony. If the shradh is not performed, the soul will continue to wander aimlessly from place to place, finding no abode or solace, suffering all the time, unable to take birth as another being on earth, you know. I think that's what's happened with his father too; his soul is not finding any peace anywhere nor can enter a new body. So now it is bothering us instead. All the sufferings of the soul end only after the shradh is performed, at which time, the soul can enter the body of another being; in other words, it incarnates on earth as a different individual."

"Sorry I don't understand? How is his father bothering you? He's dead, isn't he?"

I interrupted, "Well, uh, it is a bit more complicated than that." Then I came close to my mother and whispered to her that we should not disclose anything about what we'd been experiencing since these last few days. Then, in an attempt to distract the mind of our guest and entertain him a bit, I told Mr. Zant, "You know, I remember how Mom used to tell me an interesting thing about this shradh ceremony: that the Brahmins who accept the invitation of this food offering ceremony of shradh also share in the sins of the deceased. Like, say, if the deceased had committed one hundred sins in his entire lifetime and you offer food to one hundred Brahmins, then each Brahmin gets a share of those sins in the ratio of 'one sin per head'".

"Well, that sure IS interesting," Mr. Zant said, poker-faced.

As a matter of fact, I never used to believe in those superstitions anyway; only Mom did. I don't think even my father believed in them.

"That's true. You want some tea?" Mom asked the guest.

"And I'd like it too." I added. Mom then went into the kitchen and a few minutes later, came rushing toward me, all freaked out.

"What happened?" By then I had figured that whatever had happened was bad enough to rattle an otherwise calm person like her.

"Your father's white tea cup - it's not there."

"Well? But where could it go. Its' been there since the day my father died. Have you checked the corner of the kitchen's shelf?" my aim was to normalize the situation in front of our guest, even though I had an inkling of what might have happened.

"I checked everywhere in the kitchen. When I say it's not there, it's not there. Go check yourself," my mom slumped on the floor, with her hand on her head.

I went inside the kitchen and indeed the cup wasn't there. Outside, the sun was struggling to shine and it was still foggy at places. On top of that, a cold breeze was blowing too. I opened the door facing our little garden. A combined shriek of two voices: one that of my father and another of someone I couldn't recognize, rattled me; this was followed by a quick vision of a shadowy figure whose tail was all that I could see before it vanished - after which, the tea cup fell down on the ground from atop our grown up common bean tree - and smashed! I was flabbergasted. He used to love this particular tree a lot; he would water it whenever he had time. He used to tell us how common beans were one of the most nutritious veggies available to us by virtue of Nature. He would drink tea in the intervals when he was worn out from his gardening work and often would keep his empty cup on top of this bean plant until he found time to wash it. He'd probably done the same even now; only this time Mother Nature decided against it. I came back to mumble the whole story to my mom.

Our guest looked at me with a blank stare, unable to figure what I was saying, then he went into the bathroom. I felt relieved that I didn't have to lie to him again. Every time I looked at him it kinda gave me a creepy feeling; my intuition said that he was hanging around for something else other than a mere city tour for which he could have just as well hired a professional. However, I was too busy to even ask him anything; "If he's forgotten the purpose of his visit, good for me," I said to myself, "I am already loaded with enough work as it is - don't want any more."

As we didn't know how to perform the necessary rites ourselves, the next best option for us was to hire a suitable priest for the job.

We continued to live as usual - the only unusual thing was that from then on we would keep all the lights of the apartment, excluding the kitchen, burning - both literally and figuratively - throughout the night. The clattering of utensils also continued at the usual time. One night when our guest was in the other room, Mom mumbled to me that the shradh needed to be done as quickly as possible because she was afraid that if we continued to live the way we were living, she could foresee a huge power bill at the end of the month. Then she added, "No matter what happens, we can't lose hope." One morning, out of the blue, she bolted my father's room in the upper story for reasons best known to her; other than the kitchen, it was the only part of our apartment that remained dark at night. We were afraid of the inevitable, though occasional power cuts, so that we'd always keep two LED flashlights by our side.

****

When I visited the home of our regular priest, his wife told me that he had left home on some urgent business. I asked her if she knew anybody else who'd be good enough for performing a shradh ceremony and she told me to come tomorrow when her husband was expected to arrive. I was getting impatient, however; I was even more eager than my mom about ending this menace.

"I can't wait that long." I said, as I turned my body to face the street, ready to take leave of her.

"Is it THAT urgent?"

I turned my face toward her again, "You bet."

"Your best bet is to come tomorrow." she said and went back inside her room.

I then asked around for a priest suitable for performing the shradh ceremony. On hearing my voice and then noticing me, a fat man came out of his house, walked on to his porch - where I was standing - and said that he'd be happy to help me out if he weren't bogged down by the community's marriage ceremonies. He then offered me the address of a very good priest he knew who, he said, was adept at such things. He added, however, that the priest was extremely busy all the time and had a reputation of charging higher than normal fees. I said it was okay and that I would be able to manage the rest. The address belonged to an area which I had never visited in my life before.

There was a book fair held on the lawn which I'd have to cross in order to reach my destination. The lawn was filled with plastic and paper bags, probably dumped there by the book fair visitors. The only way to cross the book fair lawn - because it was fenced on all the other sides by barbed wire - was to walk through a makeshift tunnel-like passageway made of bamboos and some striped cloth of red, white and yellow colors. To me, that struck as rather strange. Four lads of my age were strolling inside that tunnel, laughing and chatting among themselves. I asked them about the location of this priest's house and each gave me a different direction. The tunnel had exits on four sides. As I left the tunnel through its eastern exit in search of the priest, I could hear the boys laughing at my back. Eventually, after a couple of failed attempts, I was back at the tunnel and it was then that I realized how they'd taken me for a fool and were messing with me. By then I'd grown a little wiser so instead of asking those rapscallion dudes again, I preferred to ask a middle-aged man about the location of the priest's house. He told me to walk straight through the northern exit of the tunnel, then turn left and walk straight again until the lawn ended, upon which I should come across an under-construction building, where I would notice a parked bicycle. 'His house is just beside that building you see over there', he added, pointing his finger at the distant building.

I related the entire tale to the priest as soon as I met him. Even before he could offer anything to my father's soul, the priest had already started offering me various excuses about why he would be unable to help me. After much cajoling and begging, he agreed to do the job for about two thousand rupees. I said that was a fairly big amount and that I needed to talk to my mom about it as I didn't have her permission to make any deal above one thousand with any stranger without asking her first.

"If you ain't prepared to spare even that much for your loving father who did everything for you, then I am really disappointed in you. Today's kids, huh!' He talked about my father with such confidence as if he'd known us for years!

"I'd like to ask you something."

"Yeah? Go ahead. I can answer anything related to shradh "

"What is this connection with the clattering of utensils, can you tell?"

"The utensils?" he stroked his chin for a while, "Are you sure your father's apparition is actually doing it?"

"Yes, very much. I am confident about it."

"Tell me something then, was he a great foodie?"

"Oh yes, he was as much obsessed with food as he was with gardening."

"Oh I see. What do you guys cultivate?"

"Veggies, mostly."

"And what was it your father loved to eat most?"

"Veggies. Why?"

"Well I think your father's soul is hungry. He is probably scrounging for food in the kitchen."

"What?? That's ridiculous."

"It is not, not for the believers."

"Well, I hope the shradh takes care of it."

"It would, definitely; that's what it is for!" he said, with a snide smile.

The same night Mr. Zant came to me and said, "Can I ask you a favor?"

"Oh man, can't you hold on your city tour for a while longer? You can see well how BUSY we're now. I hardly have time to breathe, let alone fool around. How can anybody be so INSENSITIVE?"

"Calm down son. He might have something important to say."

"Mom, he is just obsessed with touring the city that's all."

"No, not that. I just wanted to say, whatever happened to your father was unfortunate. He was a good man."

"Oh, that...yeah, well, it was so sudden, but thanks."

"The real reason why I am here is because of a contract I hoped to get passed through your father. I need it quick. I know you're getting annoyed, but I am in a real hurry about it."

Here comes another headache, I thought. "Oh, what contract?"

"Well? Maybe you don't know about this, but I need this cash advance urgently so that I can set up my clothing business in this city; the one reason why I agreed to the city-tour invitation. But really, I had heard a lot about your father from my circle. He was kind enough to take up the responsibility of expediting the whole process for some of my colleagues. You know, the red tape here in this city is so big, I have heard that it can take the little guy more than six months to set up a new business here if he prefers to proceed through the usual route. A friend told me that with your father's help people get contracts like these processed in a matter of a few days, which's why..."

"You're here?," my mother asked, "That was his hobby, sort of. I am guessing a lot of people are going to feel the pinch now."

"He'd connections with the man and his chair. Now I'd need to renew them to help you," I said, adding, "is it some small business, uh, government grants stuff, huh? I think I saw a contract like that in the pile Mom gave me."

"Yes. Not a grant, but cash advance for small businesses like mine, handed out by the government. It is a new scheme and there is a big difference: a grant does not need to be repaid. However, as per law only non-profits are eligible to receive grants."

"Oh, don't' worry about it. It is with me; you can be rest assured - I will get it done. Right now I am kinda feeling down so I ask that you lay low about it for a while. Not to be mean, but I'd like to make it clear to you: I am not my father okay? *I* didn't promise you anything, ergo, I owe you nothing. That said, I'll look into it as soon as I start feeling a little better."

"Don't be rude Son."

"Oh, I can understand. It's all right man. But the contract is void after fifteen days just so you know. I got to get it submitted within that time frame. I hope I can get the loan soon. Getting a new contract from those bureaucrats is quite another headache, I hope you understand."

"Oh, I am sure you would get it way before that. Like I said you can stay here for some time."

"Thanks Man."

After some dawdling, my mother managed to collect the money by withdrawing from her meager bank savings and asking for temporary loans from her friends in the neighborhood. She said she felt a little embarrassed at having to beg 'Like THAT!,' even if from her friends, because she'd never done so in her whole life, "Nobody knows where sometimes some circumstances bring you to," she said, and that she didn't feel nearly as bad when withdrawing her own bank money. She told me that no matter what our financial difficulties might be, the shradh must be performed immediately, at all costs, or else we would continue to live in nightmares.

A day later, during the hours of twilight, a dark-shadowy figure approached us, ostensibly in order to attack me and Mom. I had a kitchen knife in my hand, which I was going to use to chop some veggies in the kitchen. As soon as I brandished the knife at it, the figure escaped after making a quick U-turn, then a long stride; I could recognize it by its tail. I thought that was odd; I didn't know that even ghosts were terrified of sharp objects. Why should they be - I wondered - if they indeed lacked any kind of physical form like us, what harm could then a knife do? Or was it the glaze of stainless steel that terrified him as would even the last rays of sunlight - probably??

It was certainly not my father's apparition - I was sure of that. I couldn't figure out why it haunted us like that.

In desperation and anxiety my mom asked around about these weird episodes. After she described to them all that was happening, in every minute detail, the neighbors were unanimous about one thing: that a shradh ceremony would end all our woes.

****

The ceremony was taking place in our courtyard. We had built a square-shaped fire pit of four-by-four size. The priest was chanting various mantras which obviously meant absolutely zilch to us. I was standing and watching the whole thing there, along with Mr. Zant. Mom was in her room; she said she didn't want to be any part of it. I was, on my part, just concerned about ending the menace, once and for all. The priest then started offering liquid ghee to the consecrated fire burning in the fire pit - using a ladle he held in his right hand.

"What's he doing?" Mr. Zant asked me.

"It's called homa, a type of yagna."

"What's yagna?"

"The process through which you make an offering to the gods above. This is how you do it to appease them."

It was odd that every time he chanted some deity's name and poured ghee into the fire, a shadowy figure would appear in front of us - the same one with the tail - riding along the front wall of our house, chased by that mist-like figure of my father. The fact that it was daytime didn't seem to have any effect on them - or so it seemed. I asked the priest about this strange phenomenon, but he ignored me and continued doing what he was doing. Perhaps the ritual was supposed to be carried on uninterrupted, I thought. Soon after, the apparitions vanished into the wall and I started hearing different shrieks coming from various directions, one of which seemed a little familiar to me. A shivering Mr. Zant held my hand with both his hands, as if I could protect him in any way.

My mom panicked this time and came rushing out of her room toward me. "What's happened, Son?" she said, wailing. Evidentlyshe'd heard those shrieks too. But I remained calm and started consoling her. I couldn't figure out whether she was weeping out of fear or sorrow. Then I heard a shriek, clearly resembling the voice of my father. At the same time, I saw that same dark shadowy figure once again, this time, walking in very long strides across the wall in a way that resembled floating; it was as if the wall meant nothing to it; once again it was followed by the same white, mist-like apparition of my father. They both vanished as they reached the door. The priest then asked me to offer a pinda. I asked Mom, "Where have you kept those rice balls? We need them now."

"Oh, I see. I have them in the kitchen. I'll be bringing them in a minute."

The priest yelled, "We would also need a bowl of water in addition."

"Hopefully the vermin haven't eaten them up." I joked, as she rushed toward her kitchen and our guest chuckled a bit.

"Rice balls? For what?" Mr. Zant asked.

"Rice balls made by mixing barley with cooked rice, black sesame seeds and ghee."

"What for?"

"The priest asked for pinda, didn't you hear?"

"Hey fella, I can't wait for too long," the priest was getting a bit impatient, apparently, "I got to go to other places. Is your mother coming or what?"

"Yeah Sir, don't worry. She'd be here in a minute just as she said."

"I see. So is it food for this priest?" Mr. Zant continued unabatedly.

"Nope. It is food for my father's soul."

I was confused myself so I asked the priest about the whole phenomenon I had been witnessing all throughout the ritual.

He asked me for his fees first; I thought that was unfair because the shradh ceremony was yet to be completed, not that I had much of a choice so I paid him reluctantly. After the payment, he explained to me that someone else's hungry soul was bent on snatching away anything that was offered to my father, which was why he'd been shadowing my father's ghost; my father was chasing him away so that he could get the pinda himself instead of the same being stolen from him by that evil dark shadowy figure. I then asked him if my assumption was correct that the mist-like figure was indeed my father and the priest replied in the affirmative. It made me a little sad when I realized how he was getting tormented even after his death; I used to believe that all pains of a man ended with his death on earth.

Soon my mother arrived with two bowls: one full of water, the other one containing rice balls.

The priest then instructed me on how to offer the pinda to my father's departed soul. As I extended the bowl containing the pinda balls in one hand and another bowl full of water, two cold, white hands immediately grabbed them from me. Even though the hands didn't touch me, I could still feel a sort of cold breath. Soon after receiving the bowls, the mist-like figure vanished. There was no trace of that other shadowy figure either.

"Would these ghosts bother us again?" I asked the priest.

"No, not for now, but the menace's not ended yet."

"What do you mean?" Then I turned to my mother and whispered to her, "This whole thing's been quite a headache." The priest seemed to have overheard us. He turned to me and told me that I'd have to go through this same 'headache' every month of the following year. I asked him, "Will this never end, then?" He said that it would definitely end at the end of the year when I would have to perform this ritual again in order to complete the process. As he was walking away, he told me not to forget to feed the Brahmins, gift them nice clothes and anything else possible.

I followed him, all the while asking about how I could know if the ritual had been successful.

Eventually, he turned to me and replied, "Why? You don't have faith in me? Then why did you call on me?"

"No, that's not what I meant." I fumbled a bit.

The priest then smiled, "You are quite a curious kid. Turn your back: a few grains from the rice bowl you'd offered to your father have fallen on the ground: tell me what do you see?"

"Yeah," I said, "I see a bunch of crows eating those rice grains."

"Which means that the ceremony has been duly fulfilled. Crows eating rice grains on such an occasion is a good omen, got it?"

But don't crows eat rice grains anyway, I wondered. However, before I could pose any further questions to him, the priest had vanished from my eyesight. Boy, that was quite a fast walk, I concluded.

Just then Mr. Zant tapped on my shoulder, "Hello, do you think you can look into my contract now?"

***

I woke up to a clean'n'clear morning the next day - full of sunshine. I mumbled, "Contract? Umm, maybe...umm, Mom, what happened to Zant's contract?"

"Who? Get up, you got a lot of work to do. In a while your father would be returning from the market and ask for tea. The utensils have to be washed and ready before that, especially your father's white tea cup. Got it?" She was walking away but stopped midway as if she remembered something just then, "You didn't seem to have eaten those rice balls I'd made for you yesterday. SLEPT HUNGRY?

I made those balls especially for you with ghee, black sesame seeds...and now they have become COLD...come on, you don't have much time left now for chit-chat, you know. Your father could be back here any minute; he'd be in special hurry as he has unfinished business contracts left since last night...better GULP those balls if you're hungry because you gotta get to work quick."

"WHAT??? Aww, shit." I mumbled. Confused and somewhat relieved at the same time, I asked my mother, "Father'd be returning?? You sure? What about the shradh?"

"What shradh?"

Acknowledgments (people who helped make my story what it is):
Graham Brand
Geoff Worboys
Jim Bowering

Author: Marlowe Sr.,

Dave

"Hey, what's up guys?" I asked the first guy, as I took a seat next to him.

Those two white guys: they were generally reserved, keeping to themselves and chatting in English which was enough to tell me they were foreigners. The natives can be brown, yellow, or black, but they certainly cannot be white, that's for sure; not to mention that we don't speak impeccable English like them either - well, we can't, to be specific. I was quite eager to have a tete-a-tete with them, but at the same time, I was also hesitating a bit, as they didn't seem to be quite sociable initially when they boarded the train. In fact, as soon as they'd boarded the train, they sat on the floor, even though the compartment's seats were mostly empty (it being a public holiday). Half-an hour later, however, they sat on the seats at the extreme end of the compartment.

The train halted at a station as I had just started smoking my cigar and looking at the sights through the window. An ostensibly blind, fat female beggar boarded the compartment. Soon enough, she started asking for handouts. Unlike a normal blind person she was blinking a lot - perhaps to hide her normal eyesight. Other fake beggars would at least make an effort to LOOK fake by taping their eyelashes with some kind of transparent adhesive, but not this woman. I left my seat and stood near the entrance of the compartment in order to get a breath of fresh air; the weather was so hot that I felt somewhat suffocated. Sometime later I realized that the two white foreigners had paid her a decent sum of money, which explained why she didn't beg anything more from anyone else in that compartment and moved straight for the next one in a rather easy gait which again proved to me that she was not really blind. I wish I knew they'd be that dumb; I could have tried warning them against this cheat then. It was then that I walked up to them.

"Yeah, hello?" said the first guy.

"Mind if I ask you guys a question?"

"Sure, go ahead."

"Where are you guys from?"

"We're Russians."

"Oh. And, I think you belong to the Krishna cult right?"

"Krishna Consciousness," the second guy corrected me, as he fondled his Mridangam drum a bit with his hand.

"How did you know?" the first guy asked, with a subtle, crooked smile.

"Well your shaved head, except for that lock of hair at the back of your head, your attire - you know, those white dhotis and kurtas you're wearing, your chanting of the Hare Krishna mantra off and on, and that drum..."

They both laughed boisterously. "We've more to show, ha ha," the second guy said as he whipped out a red pocketbook form his pocket. I thought he would show me a Bible, but it was Bhagavad Gita. Then they asked, "And what're you into?"

The train halted at a station, and out of the many passengers who boarded it, there was a kerchief peddler too. Right away, he entered our compartment with his huge bag full of purple kerchiefs and started peddling, "This is the BEST kerchief you would ever find for the price. I will be getting down on to the next station. If you want, you better take it now. Time is running fast. You may touch the kerchief with your hand, but you will get it only after you pay the cash. Once I get down to the next station no one else will offer you such 100%-cotton purity, no matter how much you pay. For only Rs.60, this is rather a cut-throat deal." He then reiterated the whole thing again, and again.

"ME? I am into the religion called NOTHING."

They both smiled. The first guy asked, "What's that supposed to mean?"

One of the co-passengers joked, "Wow, what a great dielog. He is giving great dielogs." He meant 'dialog' of course. The one sitting

117

beside him added, "Who even knows for sure if these kerchiefs are even 100% cotton or made of voile?"

"Now, look, Sir, now I simply HAVE to raise my voice on this issue," the kerchief peddler said, apparently a little pissed-off, "I must, given the kind of things you are saying...it is not like I'm making a big profit with this business. You didn't even feel the thing with your hand and you are already making accusations. Now if I say something, you'd say I am bad. That's the way it goes" The two started laughing even more loudly, almost falling over each other, until the kerchief peddler resumed his peddling.

The kerchief seller then approached me. I ignored him and continued chatting with the foreigners.

"Well, it is just that I am into no religion because I don't believe in gods because I am an atheist." I said the whole thing in one breath; I thought it was the longest sentence I'd spoken in my life in that fashion.

"What?" The first guy squeaked a little.

By now the kerchief seller had almost shoved his kerchief on to my lap. Perhaps that was his way of persuading me to buy something from him, but I found it a rather rude gesture. I gave him a dirty look upon which he took the kerchief off me; the next thing I knew was that he walked to the next compartment, but not before trampling my feet with his sneakers in a way that seemed accidental but I knew was deliberate.

"Atheist."

"What??" he asked again.

The second guy said, "He meant a-theist, I think..."

"Sorry I talk a bit fast guys. So what brings you to India? You're here for some vacation or what?"

"Well, actually, a nice vacation to India is part of the package but we're really here for proselytizing."

The first guy turned left and asked a co-passenger as the train halted midway, "How far is the StationA?"

The co-passenger apparently couldn't speak English, so he only gestured with his hand, asking them to sit tight and wait. I chimed in, "Not too far, but you guys sit still because any train that halts here can

118

take about as little as ten minutes to as long as half-an hour before it starts moving again."

"That's funny," the first guy chuckled.

"Well yeah, I guess you can blame the cabin man for the mimanagement. Nothing moves fast enough in this country, heh. How long have you been here?"

"We landed only yesterday."

"Well, you've got a lot to pass through," I chuckled, trying to appear a little smart to them. "Oh shit, I forgot to ask you the most important thing."

"What is that?"

"Your name? What's your name?"

"Oh ho, ho, ho,", the first guy laughed so hard at the question that I could hardly believe it, "Davedas."

"Are you for real? That's the name of the alcoholic protagonist of a famous eponymous novel of India..."

"Hehe. Well, actually, my real name is Dave. I got the -das added after the conversion."

"Okay Dave, I'll call you Dave then. Do you mind?"

"Nope."

"You know what, I hope you don't mind, but you shouldn't have really paid that fat woman; she wasn't really blind, you know; I can tell. It is a common vocation taken up by the slobs here who don't want to work for a living; this country is full of it. People who are really, I mean, REALLY blind, have got more self-respect than those A-holes; they seldom beg."

They merely looked at each other and looked a bit oddly at me, twitching their eyebrows a little.

"Tell me something - honestly, do you at all like the weather here? I mean, with this intolerable heat..."

"The place we come from is actually hotter in summer."

"You're kidding. I thought Russia was colder..."

"Depends on where you live. It is a HUGE country with varied weather."

"Well, I am sure about this one thing...uh, I've heard there are a lot of hot Caucasian chicks in there. Tell me if I am wrong on this one too. Of course you people probably miss all the fun."

"Excuse me?"

"I mean, you guys are celibates right?"

"We have wives," the two said jointly. Dave added, "Celibates don't wear whites. They wear saffron only."

"Oh, I see, " well that proves how little I know about this cult, I thought, "so, what is your religion all about? I don't know a lot about it so if you don't mind enlightening me a little...I was just born a Hindu by the way."

"Well, it is not a lot different from your religion...I mean, it is basically Hinduism in its most conventional, traditional form. You cannot partake in any form of addictive stuff, meat, fish, etc., for one. And you cannot use violence to..."

"Well, that's odd. Even Sri Krishna advocated manslaughter for the purpose of upholding truth and religion, whatever that shit meant at that time. "

"Oh, we didn't know that."

Dumb western people brainwashed by the media and those religious fanatics out there, I thought; they are so gullible that they might as well readily believe it if someone tells them Sri Krishna never killed anybody in his lifetime - no matter how much full of shit that might be. This cult seems to be a new fad going in the West these days; someday, one might even notice mass conversions to Islam or Buddhism, not that it would make much of a difference. People who are disillusioned with one religion hop on to another in hope of gaining something more; they have a right to, but I truly believe that in the end, all religions are more or less basically the same; it is not so much the religion but the person joining it and his nature, that really matter in the end. If he wants to make a difference in his life or the life of others, *he" needs to change, *he* needs to take the right actions, *his* attitude has to be cordial, otherwise changing a religion is not much different than changing our clothes, unless we don't change our true self. If indeed we change our true self, then we can make a difference with ANY religion, or even no religion at all. "You know how he died? It's quite an interesting story."

"What're you saying?" the second guy looked at me, puzzled, "The Supreme Lord doesn't die. He can't die. He is beyond all forms of life and death."

"Yeah, right," I said sarcastically, "that's what you believe huh? EVERYBODY has to die," I said.

"All we know is that," Dave started, "a time came when he thought that his work on earth was over and then he, being an incarnation of our Supreme Lord, left his mortal remains on earth."

"Well, in a way you are right, but the story goes that once this hunter actually mistook Krishna's heel, who was at the time sitting underneath a tree, for a deer and aimed his arrow at him. Krishna, however, forgave him and said it was all pre-ordained to happen that way, before He ascended to heaven."

"Well, that's odd," the second guy smiled a bit, then twitched his forehead, "how can anyone mistake a human ankle for an animal?" He then started caressing the two apertures of the drum with his hands.

I snapped my fingers, "Well, that...that is the story buddy."

We finally reached our destination and all the three of us disembarked on to the StationA's platform. As we walked, I said, "Don't you guys carry cymbals?"

"Oh yes," said Dave, as he put his fingers in his pocket to whip out the couple.

"Nice. Can I try them, uh..." as I forwarded my hand.

"Sure, go ahead and play a little if you want to."

I could hear some shouts and warnings from a man but was too engrossed in the chat to bother. A fat handcart puller approached us from the opposite direction with his loaded handcart and rammed the second guy hard on his flank before running away with his handcart, saying "Told you, told you to get outta my way". He looked like some mammoth giant, a force of fury perhaps. The guy fell on the edge of the platform; an inch further and he would have found his body lying on the railway tracks.

"God, some people can be so blind," the second guy grumbled.

Dave asked, "You hurt?"

I asked, "You okay?"

"I'll live. Just got a bit hurt on my kneecap, will be all right."

"You have seen nothing yet buddy. This is one of the filthiest and most crowded stations in this state. I mean, look at them dogs loitering here and there on the platform; ready to devour on any food leftovers dumped by the passengers before boarding the train. Where are you actually headed to?"

"Krishnanagara."

" Krishnanagara, the city? You wanna start preaching there?"

"Actually, we've heard that there are a lot of Sri Krishna temples over here - about fifty-one. We plan to visit them all, get the Lord's blessings before beginning our journey."

"Very well then but you are in the wrong place buddy. You boarded the wrong train. You actually need to go to Station B which is on the other side of the Ganges. You ain't got no train coming here that would take you to Krishnanagara. Now you got to board a bus from here, land at Station B to catch a train, etc..."

"Oh, we didn't know that. Our group advisor said this was the way to go so we did and..."

"Well, your group advisor was wrong and what I am telling you is the real deal. You wanna get going or prefer to waste time arguing here with me? I was going someplace else." I glanced at my wrist watch, "but uh, I guess it can wait; I can go there later on. If you want I can drop you at your destination before resuming my journey."

"Thank you, that is very kind of you."

We walked toward the bus terminal, passing by a blind bamboo basket maker weaving a new one. He is a regular there: he is as much an integral feature of the station as the crowd. I tossed a one rupee coin on his lap; he stopped his work and looked up; that is a kind of regular habit of mine.

***

"Okay, so it is already fifteen minutes since we've been sitting on this bus; do you know when would it leave?"

"No, I am not its driver." The two laughed at this. I actually wanted to say "I am not its goddamn driver" but figured that'd appear to be a little nasty.

"Actually, you need to have patience in this country. You know how the train crawled? The buses may not leave even after half-an-hour from its terminal; to be honest, they have no fixed departure time, or even if they have any, they don't care. They depart only when they are fully overcrowded. Told you there's a lot for you to see here..."

"Why is that?" Dave asked, as he fished out a water bottle from his cloth bag and started gulping.

"Well, it is so because," I took a deep breath, "Bus owners here pay extremely low to the staff. The pay is usually a few pennies per passenger, so they try to accommodate as many passengers as possible, to the point of overcrowding the bus."

"This must cause a lot of distress to the passengers," Dave said.

"Yeah, in a moment it would cause distress even to US," I chuckled a bit, "Anyway, what do they care?"

The driver entered the bus about fifteen minutes later when the bus was almost packed to the full, thumped his ass on his seat, fired up the engine and revved a little before moving a few yards, then stopped.

"Does he intend to depart the terminal at all?" the second guy mumbled.

***

The bus ticket collector, aka, conductor, started collecting bus fare tickets, and in time, approached us too. I preferred to pay for the three of us as I thought that language might prove to be a barrier between my foreigner co-passengers and the conductor. He, however, promptly asked me who the other two tickets were meant for.

I hesitated a little at first, then pointed my finger at my two co-passengers who were sitting beside me. The conductor quipped, "They gotta pay extra," in his native tongue, then turned to Dave and said, in English, "Pay me Rs.50, EACH of you," pointing his finger at his face the whole time.

"But isn't the going rate Rs.20 per person?" I asked.

"I ain't TALKING to you!" he switched back to his native tongue.

The two men didn't say anything and promptly paid what they were asked to pay. I wondered if they realized that they were over being overcharged. In any case, I didn't tell one more word after that because I didn't want to create a scene there.

***

So we were where we wanted to be - almost near StationB. The bus wasn't allowed to go any further than that due to the 'no-entry zone'

123

thing, so we started walking the rest of the way. We walked through a street filled up with dog shit, cow dung, filth like food leftovers and packets, illegal squatters, elderly men and women driven out of their homes, refugees and beggars - with their makeshift homes and tents. The homes were mostly made of salvaged materials: torn clothes, tin sheets, hay, tangled jute ropes, rubber sheets, etc., stuff you'd get in any trash bin here. Some had even set up mosquito nets across the sidewalk. There is nobody to poke noses into their affairs; the street is like their goddamn owned house; the pedestrians say nothing, the cops harass 'em to get their piece of the pie and the government does nothing. We walked through filthy slums with naked kids roaming around on the street. The air was filled with foul odor and the constant loud honking of automobiles. We had barely crossed a few yards when a young boy of about fifteen or sixteen years started following us. I didn't realize it until he started yelling "Hello Brahmins! Brahmins!" which made me realize that they might be referring to the two foreigners walking with me as their attire somewhat matched that of a Hindu Brahmin priest. I stopped, so did they. The boy didn't even look at me and immediately started conversing with the two foreigners in broken English. Considering his uncouth attire I had initially taken him for a thief or snatcher; there have been quite a few of them springing up in the city lately whose modus operandi is to gain the confidence of a gullible foreigner before robbing him in broad daylight. But soon his conversations made me suspicious.

"I got some good stuff for you. Making you high okay? You know? You want some high?"

"What high? What've you got" Dave asked.

"We got some brown stuff, white stuff, you know, and green stuff too. Totally pure shit."

"They don't understand these vague terms," I told him in his native tongue, "So you better be straight if you want them to buy anything."

He looked left and right, then whispered something into Dave's ears and Dave in turn whispered the whole thing to me, "He is talking of smack, coke, grass. We would have none of these, you know that. Let's go."

I told the boy in his native tongue that we don't need any of his shit and started walking toward our destination. The boy followed us. "This is pure stuff Sir , totally pure," he yelled, "ain't be getting such shit anywhere else in the city. Pretty cheap too. I can give you a sample here if you like, no money if it don't make you high," he said as he fished out small rolled paper resembling an ordinary cigarette from his pocket. By now I was getting irritated with the boy and figured that he must be gotten rid of, somehow.

I asked the two fellas to drag him along by his limbs. The boy started screamed quite a lot "Hey, where the hell YOU taking me uh? Let go of me. Don't you know I got folks down here?? CHIMO! CHIMO!" . Pretty soon, two young men started following us. Another bald man appeared on my left with a switchblade and would have taken me by surprise if not for Dave who alerted me. I soon raised an alarm as I knew I was in the proximity of the police station. I was so embarrassed by the incidents of that day that I started feeling ashamed of my nationality; I also felt a little sad at how gullible foreigners were being treated in my country; I wondered what they would be telling their families back home when they return?

After handing the boy over to the cops, we resumed our journey. We still had about a quarter of the distance to cover, but I could already see the brightly illuminated red lights of Station B. In front of the station's entrance was a huge barricade - of illegally parked cabs and auto rickshaws, waiting for passengers to board as they exit the station; one would have to move like a serpent through the mess to reach the station. I realized it was dusk even as Dave asked me, "How far is it?" I pointed the illuminated Station B to them and said my goodbyes, for no longer I had any strength left in me to accompany them any further. I sure was in no mood to know what else my countrymen were capable of; sometimes, ignorance is bliss as they say.

I'd walked only a few yards when I heard them shout at my back, "This sure is an interesting country. Lots of people here who need Lord's help for sure. Glad we came."

Guilty Comfort

By Eve Gaal

During moments of comfort,

Breeze and sun--

The distant rumble

From the military base

Quakes my chaise,

Reminding me that

Butterflies and puppies have not

Overtaken the world

With blissful kisses--

Shared photos--

Slobbering yelps--

and declarations of love.

Not yet anyway.

Kitty videos numb the pain

But blood flows on shifting sand,

Into old sewers,

on newspaper headlines,

Grasping anything amid slumping

readership.

Slurping up

Desperate wreckage,

Stunning orange flames,

Unsurpassed plasma quality--

Scared faces of running, screaming, burning,

Frightened children....

Children who

Hold marketing dollars--

While bulldozers turn Earth.

Pulling my shade--

I hide like an anxious bunny.

My tears won't solve anything,

So I offer prayers

In shamefaced comfort.

Outside the daisies sway.

Spinster's Dirge

She hung on his every word.
You've seen fruit about to fall from a tree,
They dance in the breeze
Rhythmically hesitating,
perhaps anticipating the splatter of juices on pavement.
The separation from limb
Begins at birth
Until someone deems it perfect.

It's quiet in the orchard,
Bare trees tremble,
perhaps attempting to wave.
The lucky ones are gone--
Picked over,
Those forgotten, shudder,
Cling to leaves for comfort,
Until a gust takes the bruised
Back to soil for fertilizer.

Will he call?
Is 'next time' even a compost heap of possibility?
Will someone, someday see perfection?
Sour tears water her hopeful dreams
Where love sticks to her body
Dripping, enticing and fulfilling her longing.
He's there,
Holding her trunk,
knees against her side.

Warm breath,
becoming heavier.
He pulls and plucks the ripest fruit,
and hangs on every word.

Worn
By Eve Gaal

Alone,
I hear the world chirp outside the window-
I recall holes in my underwear—
Because I have to do something-
Anything is better than nothing.
Erosion prompts movement.
Eventually I will move from this chair--
Whether I want to--or not.

I will wear a bra again,
Shave my legs,
Smile again--
As if, all is fine.
My hands quiver,
I glance around the room
But the chirping gets unbearable,
I toss my panties in the trash.

The world continues to call,
Gently, like soft voices luring prey.
My saturated heart still beats,
Fear apparent.
I push into the blinding sun to exit.

Now at the discount superstore,
buying underwear.
Three distasteful white pairs to a pack--
The painful part:
Recalls designer lace
The scratchy memories of lingerie.
Folded into tissue paper,

Wrapped like fourteen –karat gold.
Sensual to someone—once.

Checkout lady wishes me a nice day.
On my way home
The car radio has to be off.
No melancholy song is going to make me cry.

Safe at my desk
Tiny birds teeter on the branch--
I would smile,
But violent wind
Tore and shredded the nest....
They chirp
And sound happy.
The gardener raked it up.
They will move--
Whether they want to--or not.

Dancing For God
By Eve Gaal

Miriam left her coat at home and felt chills running down her back, as she crossed the parking lot from her car. Feeling frozen to the bone, she began thinking about how her warm, snuggly coat was hanging safe and well protected in her hallway closet. She also forgot to bring anything to eat, because planning ahead took extra initiative when time seemed to be so limited and traffic so heavy. Maturity had the added disadvantage of a fading memory, but she also lived a little farther than everyone else. Maybe tomorrow she'd remember these important details, she thought, pulling open the stage door. The ladies and young girls were all there when she arrived, practicing their steps and pulling on their toe shoes. Some of them were working on their hair and makeup. Others were working with the costume lady regarding their outfits or misplaced sequins.

Miriam had no sequins because she played St. Bernadette's poor peasant mother. Her outfit had to look plain and French provincial. The earthy colors and practical skirt didn't have the lift of the lead dancer playing Bernadette. It didn't have the tulle fluff of the spring birds, the wildflowers and the angels; in fact, the costume looked downright homely. Consisting of a rust brown skirt with a dark brown button front blouse, her ensemble had the exciting addition of a pale blue wool shawl in the last act. For a single woman her age, it definitely wasn't going to send any messages or get her noticed by the opposite sex. Of course, she never, ever even thought of anything like that. This show had a special message about prayer, love and chastity and the divine grace of God allowed her to be part of something she thought of as incredibly moving and spiritual. Best of all, it gave her a chance to dance!

It seemed that Miriam danced ever since she could remember. First as a child in front of the television and later, she danced in high school performances. Blonde and blue eyed, she had many opportunities to go dancing with gentlemen suitors who enjoyed the way she moved. Unfortunately, for Miriam, none of the dancing men were interested in sticking around and giving their heart away forever. While she wanted commitment, the male dancers wanted to change partners quickly, evoking a minuet rather than a waltz. Pretty soon, they danced off into the sunset with other partners and Miriam remained a virgin. She stopped dancing altogether. Then one magical day, the local diocese needed someone just like Miriam.

Mumbling a small prayer of thanks, Miriam decided to warm up by doing some stretches. She enjoyed kicking her long, lovely legs high into the air. Warming up made her smile from ear to ear and the other dancers noticed she seemed full of love and happiness. The auditorium had filled to capacity and the performance titled, Ballet of Our Lady of Lourdes had almost sold out. By the second act, Miriam felt a bit hungry, but reminded herself that soon the performance would be over and she could go home to eat. Besides, it was Lent. Later that evening, one of the cast members asked her to join them for a bite to eat, but she didn't have her coat and it was raining. "No, I can't tonight," she answered, running for her car where a warm, adoring Jesus waited patiently in the passenger seat. Turning over the engine, she cranked up the heater, letting the warm air dry the drops of cleansing water dripping down her pretty face.

"Thank you," she heard Him say. "Thank you for dancing for God."

Eve says poetry is: A collection of words tied together with sparks in an emotionally charged moment like a snapshot. It's like sharing a left contact lens, until you invite others who might relate, "see" your point.

Almost finished~

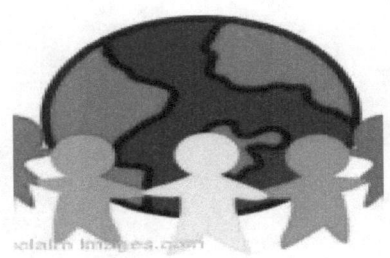

**PnPAuthors Promotion believes -
'together' we can accomplish anything.**

http://pnpauthorspattimariandpeter.ning.com/?xgi=4PBO
wIJg1TDMx7

pattimari@hotmail.com

Pulling together